BRUNO JASIENSKI

THE LEGS OF IZOLDA MORGAN

SELECTED WRITINGS

Translated by
Soren A. Gauger and Guy Torr

TWISTED SPOON PRESS

PRAGUE

2014

ISBN 978-80-86264-40-0

This publication has been funded by the
Book Institute – the ©POLAND Translation Program

CONTENTS

2 FUTURIST MANIFESTOES

TO THE POLISH NATION: A MANIFESTO
on the Immediate Futurization of Life

In full understanding that if an isolated and sporadic reform of art is divorced from life-as-such (of which every art is the pulse and organic function) it must show itself to be intrinsically hollow, fruitless and sterile, and being aware that we have made no preliminary and preparatory steps toward this reform – Polish life and art are in danger of suffocating, and the only possible and effective measure is a prompt tracheotomy – we, the Polish Futurists, hereby declare a great and radical reconstruction and reorganization of Polish life, and we call upon the citizens of the Free Polish Republic to assist us in this endeavor.

Along with the gigantic shift of states, strata, and nations, the worldwide war brought a great shift in values. The result is a culture in crisis, visible today throughout East and West Europe. This crisis has appeared in Poland in a particularly violent and unique form. A century and a half of political servitude has left a hard, indelible suture running down our physiognomy, psyche, and creative work. Our cultural consciousness has not been as free to develop as those in western states. By necessity, all our national energy chose the path of most resistance, struggling for language, life, and self-organization. In this struggle for our own national "ego," to construct a hard, unbending, all-resistant national psyche capable of surviving, Polish art became involved as well.

Standing in this city where, in an era of servitude, there arose

Polish Romantic poetry, a phantom we mercilessly hound and bludgeon, we, the Polish Futurists, pay tribute to the fact that, in our time, though the Polish nation is pulling itself together and slowly ripening, there has been no "pure" or deeply national art, written with the juice and blood of life itself, with the pulse and scream of its day, as every art can and must really be.

For these very reasons, today, as we gain an independent political existence, Polish life has entered a whole new phase, waking to a million issues at its doorstep, which there had never been time even to contemplate, but now require a swift and categorical response. Lest another wave come crashing down on us, we proclaim:

We are through with being a menagerie nation producing mummies and relics. Today, crazed and unstoppable, we are pounding on your doors and windows, screaming, clamoring, issuing demands. If we cannot devise new categories to fit the new art, an art for singing — we will not survive.

We must throw all the doors and windows open wide, air out the musty cellars, the church incense you have been taught to breathe since childhood. We are coming out to meet you, equipped with giant respirators.

We join Stanisław Brzozowski in declaring a great clearance sale of old junk. We are selling old traditions, categories, customs, pictures, and fetishes at rock-bottom prices.

A great nationwide menagerie on Wawel Hill.

We are hauling the stale mummies of the Mickiewiczes and the Słowackis out of the squares, avenues, and streets. Time to clear the pedestals, sweep out the squares, make room for the new arrivals.

We, a people of deep lungs and broad shoulders, are choking from the rank stench of your archaic messianism; we propose a new messianism, unique, modern, insane. If you don't want to be dead last in Europe — if, on the contrary, you want to be first — stop eating the West's kitchen scraps (we can afford our own menu) and you will reach the finish line in the great race of civilizations with short, synthetic strides.

Let us construct a new house for a Polish nation that has outgrown the old one. We call out to all those with life in their bones, all the misfits, all those who want to help.

We declare:

The great shifting of strata in the East and the West continues. A new force is speaking out — the conscious proletariat. All values are being reevaluated. They are pitting themselves against the whole 1,000-year-old legitimacy and illegitimacy of the culture produced on their backs, at their expense. They are being sized up against the only test in a life of struggle — hard, iron, organic labor. A great reappraisal of legitimacy is underway. If you cannot legitimize your participation in life with this all-purpose token — you will perish.

We stress the three fundamental moments in modern life: the machine, democracy, and the crowd.

The life of the intellectual strata is undergoing a slow phase of degeneration and neurasthenia. The intellectuals have outlived and digested the old categories — and new ones have yet to be created. It is a moment of wholesale crisis. Instead of being saturated with joy and dithyramb, life-as-such increasingly takes the form of a dour obligation. Modern man no longer organically enjoys life. The epidemic of suicides, human wreckage, breakdowns, and histrionics is merely a logical consequence of this phenomenon. This cannot go on. It requires immediate medical attention. Our main strategy will be:

More sunshine.

An ancient Chinese proverb says: "Carry an umbrella even when the sun is shining." With us this has organically taken root.

We are throwing away our umbrellas, hats, and bowlers, we will go with heads bare. Bare necks. Let everyone tan their skins. Houses will be constructed with glass walls to the south. More light, air, and space. If the Polish parliament met outside we would have a much sunnier constitution.

Work consumes 3/4 of modern man's energy; he needs strong and healthy food — new, vibrant, synthetic emotions. Only art, at present, can provide these emotions. Art should be the juice and joy of life, not a source of mourning or consolation. Let us break once and for all with the fictions of "pure art," "art for art's sake," and "art for the absolute." **Above all, art must be human, i.e., for the people and the masses, democratic, and universal.**

With this understanding of the role of art in addressing the issues of the day, we cry:

Artists, take to the streets!

Art that nests in the concert halls, exhibition spaces, palaces of art, etc. for a few hundred or a few thousand people is a comical and anemic monstrosity, appreciated by 1/100,000,000 of the population. Modern man has no time for concerts and exhibitions that 3/4 of the population are unable to attend. Art, therefore, must be everywhere:

Traveling poem-concerts and concerts in trains, trams, canteens, factories, cafés, squares, stations, halls, arcades, parks, from the balconies of houses, etc., etc., etc., at all times of day and night.

Art must be unexpected and all-pervasive, it must knock you off your feet.

Modern man has long abandoned his hopeful expectations. Legal codes have standardized and classified our surprises, once and for all. Life, which unlike modern machines is gloriously unpredictable, has increasingly become indistinguishable from machines. The immortal categories of logic, by which Concept A must always precede Concept B, inevitably coming together to equal Concept C, have become insupportable. The $2 \times 2 = 4$ of mathematics has grown to the dimensions of a ghastly polyp whose tentacles have spread everywhere. All of logic's capabilities have been utterly exhausted. In our time, we eternally spin in circles till we drop unconscious. For all its logic, life has become horrid and illogical.

We, the Futurists, want to show the way out of this ghetto of logic. Man has ceased to rejoice because he has ceased to expect. Only life seen as a ballet of possibilities and surprises could restore this joy to him.

On the Ferris wheel of the self-explanatory, we will explain that nothing is self-explanatory, and that beyond the one logic there is a whole sea of illogicalities, each of which could create its own distinct logic, where $A+B=F$, and 2×2 equals 777.

A deluge of wonders and surprises. Nonsense dancing in the streets. Art *is* the masses.

Everyone can be an artist.

Theaters, circuses, street performances played by the public itself.

We call all the poets, painters, sculptors, architects, musicians, and actors to take to the streets.

The stage is turning. Time to change the decor.

The walls of buildings as pictures. Multi-wall houses, round and cone-shaped. The band is playing a march. The people want to keep step.

We call upon the craftsmen, the tailors, the shoemakers, the tanners, and the barbers to create new, unseen suits, hairstyles, and costumes.

We call upon all the technicians, engineers, and chemists to come up with new and incredible inventions.

Technology is an art, just like painting, sculpture, and architecture.

A good machine is a model and the summit of the work of art, through its perfect combination of economy, precision, and dynamics. Morse's telegraph apparatus is a masterwork 1,000-times greater than Byron's *Don Juan.*

Among the architectural, visual, and technological works of art we can distinguish one — WOMAN — as the perfect reproductive machine.

Woman is an untapped and incalculable force, remarkable in her influence. We demand absolute equality for women in all spheres of life, both private and public.

Above all — equality in erotic and family relationships.

The number of married couples who live apart or are officially separated has soared to such heights as to undermine the fabric of society.

We deem the immediate introduction of divorce to be the only way to prevent and halt this process.

We hereby stress: the erotic moment is one of the most primary functions of life-as-such. This moment is an elemental and extremely important source of *joie de vivre*, under the condition that your approach to it is simple, clear, and sunny. Przybyszewski-style sexual tragedies display a lack of taste and prove the utter spinelessness and impotence of modern men. We call on women — as the physically more robust and stronger sex — to take the initiative.

In light of the above, Polish society has to control and supervise social life and production of all types, prohibiting the creation of all that is incompatible, irrelevant, or harmful. **The first essential step is to control all artistic production.** Don't let them slop their buckets of stale, senile, snobbish literature, incapable even of arousing your sexual drives. An organized audience is an irresistible force. We will allow no unnecessary books to go to print — no one needs them.

We appeal to all citizens of the Polish State to stand up in self-defense. The Polish public has outgrown its artists. Today's viewer openly yawns at *Macbeth* and feels a vague stab in the appendix watching the Eaglet's demise. Polish art is unable to supply new and nourishing sustenance. **The only effective means of combating this creative void is a joint, coordinated sabotage of all senescent literature and art. Stop going to the theaters, stop buying books, don't read magazines etc., etc., etc.**

To organize a joint effort in Polish society toward the immediate, profound, deep-rooted, fundamental, and long-lasting Futurization of life, we are establishing gigantic Futurist parties all across the Polish Republic. Any working citizen who instinctively senses this moment of cultural crisis and wants to find a way out can become an active party member. There is a whole society of these neurasthenics and martyrs in today's modern life. To them we extend our hand.

We appeal to the "new people," "untainted" by this syphilitic civilization, whom the worldwide war flushed to the surface and whom the old civilization continues to treat like bastard children. **We, the Futurists, are the first to reach out in fraternity to the "new people." They will be a fortifying, invigorating juice to rejuvenate the old, deteriorating race of yesterday's people, a painful but necessary vaccine that the great historical cataclysm has injected into a decaying prewar Europe, whose stench was beginning to rankle the nose.**

Forging through to tomorrow, our party will be unprecedented, all-encompassing, crazed. Everyone and no one can be a leader. Total decentralization. We know neither leaders nor foot soldiers, everyone is an equal worker in a struggle for survival. We are marking a great moment in the history of humanity.

Fate has outlived its usefulness and died. From this point on, everyone can create his own life and life-as-such.

We, the Futurists, are coming to the rescue of Polish society. We will answer all queries with precise guidelines in the spirit of this manifesto and with instructions in all fields. At our call, every nameless member of the Futurist Party (we don't need your names – there are only equals, conscious and present) will sound off at his post.

For any action of ours to be effective, we demand that the Polish Republic immediately declare that artists are to receive the same immunity enjoyed by parliamentary deputies. The artist represents the Nation just as well as a member of parliament – only his competencies and field of operations are different.

In this great landmark moment, we, the Futurists, will forget the old abuses, we choose to forget that all our work to date, striving in the selfsame direction, has met with a hostile, brainless, and snide response from Polish society. We know all too well that this was a misunderstanding perpetrated by misleading informants and commentators, and by the absence of a united front and a clear, tangible statement of faith from our camp. Now all these misunderstandings are clearing up all on their own. With a purple faith in tomorrow and its infinite possibilities we wipe clean all that was bad, redundant, and senile, both within and outside of us, we extend a hand to the Polish nation. If you are a living nation and not a dwarf nation, if a century and a half of enslavement has not sucked all the juice from your spines, if you are indeed the nation of tomorrow and not a parasite nation – join us.

We call on one and all to start a mass unanimous Futurist action the moment this Manifesto is made public.

Krakow, April 20, 1921

NIFE IN THE GUTT
2nd Phuturist Pamflet

30,000 kopies of the phuturist maniphesto — distributed around poland over forteen daze. gowged with this nife in the gutt, the slumbering kattel of polish art began to holler. the woond pyooked up the lava of phuturism. sityzens, help us tare the phlaid skin from yer bones. stop dragging about yer party slowgans like: "god and nayshun." the red polish phlag has long ben a red nosewipe. demokrats — raze the phlags with the werds of our swiss phriends: we want to piss **in a raynbow of kolors!**

paynted pants

In many private houzes, and sum public wonz too, like the so-kalled zachęta phine art gallery, the walz are hung with grate bloks of kanvas, vary often paynted wonz. Why dont the malishus zachęta paynters paynt there own pants, why do they hang there work on walz insted of themselves? Walking about in kolored pants theid play there part as entertainment four the peeple. The payntings hangin on the walz only feed the gossip of a duzen gazets.

As we kan see, the guverment thinks the starving poles cant be satisphied with there own art stawls, sinz itz a punishbel ofenz to take the rembrants and other rafaels out of the kuntry. We stand hear and beg: lets start a holesale kontraband, letz ship this krud overseez.

Homeowners, kover yer walz and interiors with phuturist kompozishuns.

Peeple, komishun theez paynters and skulpters, onlee hear in poland, to dekorate yer streets, skwares, and cidewalks:

tytus czyżewski, henryk gotlieb, leon chwistek, józef jarema, zbigniew and andrzej pronaszko, marian szczerbuła, kazimierz tomorowicz, zygmunt waliszewski, romuald witkowski.

We kall on all sityzens of the naishun:

Sityzens, paynt yerselvz
and yer wifz and childrin!

The last phuturist evenings in Zakopane konkluded with a fite between too fakchuns of the audyence, with phists and eggs! **The wimmin all stood behind the phuturists!** Sune the theetrs two will be phuturized! The resent multiplikation of theetrs is the best proof of there total bankruptsee. The revolted publik is demolishing the staje as we no it. Eggs are the only wepin fur the sivilized man: they seam like hand grenaids butt arent deadlee. We shake hands with frants and swisserlend. **Marinetti is a stranger to us.** Sune ther'll bee new karnivals of phuturist poetry in warsaw, in krakoof, in lvoov, in poznagn, and in all the other sities of poland, where the masses will kome two see the phamous polish phuturists

TYTUS CZYŻEWSKI, BRUNO JASIEŃSKI, STANISŁAW MŁODOŻENIEC, ANATOL STERN, ALEKSANDER WAT.

Krakow, 1921

THE LEGS OF IZOLDA MORGAN

And now I see with a sickened soul,
eyes fixed upon a scrap of sky,
that I was just a massive sow
its million teats run dry.

— "All Saints' Soccer"

EXPOSÉ

I fear there's no getting around a preface this time. Let's try to do this as gracefully as possible.

My relationship with the Polish public has sketched itself out over these last few years in an utterly clear and singular manner, and requires no commentary. Our nation has had its authors who have been liked and disliked, popular and unpopular, adored and ignored. These categories of authors have created and continue to create our so-called "literature." But apart from this "official" literature – outside its brackets, as it were – every epoch has its *poètes maudits*, who are reluctantly mentioned in passing and with evident disgust. There is nothing to be done about this. These are most commonly barbarians; they either have little appreciation for the refined game of so-called literature or stubbornly pretend not to understand it.

Let's suppose a certain society of cosmopolitans is amusing themselves by parrying subtle witticisms, and a man uninformed of such, or – even worse – ill-bred, starts to take everything that is said with the utmost seriousness. Naturally, the whole game would be ruined, the company would gather up their toys and turn their backs on the uninvited boor.

And thus it has always been.

It sometimes happens that later epochs place these ill-bred folk on pedestals and laud them, in fact, as the epitome of their generation, without paying the slightest bit of heed to society.

Sometimes the basic outlines remain the same.

It depends whether these people were guided by a truth they could not deny or simply acted out of snobbery, *pour passer le temps.*

Examples: Christ and Oscar Wilde.

We'll let history decide which of these two groups we fall into. The polemics that have appeared in our press over this issue for upward of two years have been, suffice to say, fruitless and insipid.

When, in August of 1921 in Zakopane, I was returning from an evening of reading some of my finest verses, escorted by my listeners, who for the whole length of Krupówki Street (from the Morskie Oko Hotel to the Trzaski Restaurant) pelted me with stones large enough to split open the head of an average — or even not-so-average — mortal (though it had, alas, already gotten dark), it occurred to me that the opinions of our public elite, which were being clearly expressed that evening, were to my mind . . . all too flattering. Back then, being publicly stoned was not within the scope of my ambitions. Such lavish praise made me blush. I had to admit with some embarrassment that my prior achievements had been minor, and that the public had been all too gracious. And yet this is our audience. It knows how to reward its favorites beyond their accomplishments. This does have its advantages. The author who has been selected to experience such moments of embarrassment will surely pool his strengths and will not disappoint the hopes placed in him. This is why I am so grateful to the Zakopane public for that evening, though my contribution to Polish literature was undeserving. It made me freshly aware of the direction I should take, to stay the course. And if one day I am granted the chance to experience another evening like it (and all signs seem to point in that direction), I am sure I will no longer feel abashed by such generosity.

The hostile outbursts in various Polish cities, the police breaking up my readings in Warsaw, the confiscations, the interventions by the Krakow City Council to put an end to all my readings in the Municipal Theater, the official expulsion from Krynica, where I had sought to organize a reading, because my stay there was deemed "undesirable" and not in the "interests of the Republic of Poland," the chronic removal of my posters by the public and members of parliament (Dymowski), the efforts of the Society of Young National Democrats to prevent me from reading in Lwów, and so forth — all these were signposts that I was headed down the right track.

So it would be unjust of the public to suppose that I do not value their role in my creative development. Quite the contrary — they have been a constant yardstick for my work, something like a safety valve regulating the merit of the things I produce.

In launching a new book onto the market, it seems incumbent upon me to furnish it with something like my private confessions, and this for a few reasons.

This book differs somewhat from my previous work to date, known to the "public at large," to give them their full title. Some will speak of a new phase — a step out of line, a swing to the "right" etc. I would like to reassure them all at once.

The present book fully conforms with my work like few others before it; it is by all means the sum of a minor creative period.

The fact that I have chosen the form of the novel is entirely explicable.

1. In declaring the democratization of art, it is difficult to bypass the novel as such, given that of the 15% of the Polish public who read, no doubt 14.75% read exclusively prose, while the some remaining 0.25% read poetry.

2. In struggling to cleanse Polish art of the muck, there is no getting around this particular form, it being the muckiest of all.

I do not claim that the present book should stand as an example of how the contemporary novel ought to be written. But it is most certainly an example of how the novel *cannot* be written these days (the joke that you wish to insert here, my dear reader, only confirms your naiveté).

In defiance of all my publishers who pay by the word, this book contains the number of pages you see before you (no more, no less), and its structure is made of reinforced concrete. Meandering novels that fly in the face of basic structuring principles are now — let us hope — a thing of the irretrievable past.

Today's novel can no longer be a narration of facts that evoke certain psychological states in the reader corresponding to said facts. This path is fundamentally spurious and applicable only to those readers with very primitive internal constitutions.

A contemporary novel provides the reader with the key mental states, and on their basis a range of corresponding facts may be constructed. Thus, the plot might come together differently for every reader, yielding an inexhaustible richness.

The subject matter, in this case thrilling and perverse, has no significance as such. It is macabre only to the extent that *every* issue is macabre if we choose to take it to its logical conclusion. If we spend an hour contemplating a house we pass by obliviously every day, we find this house slowly grows to ghastly dimensions. Similarly, if we stare at a single point for too long, the contours of reality begin to blur, and where a statuette once stood we might now see a cow wearing a jacket and a Chinese man.

The hectic pace of contemporary life, striving with inexorable logic, racing down a slope to a fixed point with the speed of an accelerated transmission, has created an entirely new reality, a reality of white-hot steel shuddering on the verge of hallucination.

Such is this book.

It is also the critique of a signature moment in the contemporary consciousness, which I would call a Futuristic consciousness, a result of the past decade or two.

That is all I have to say about it.

The "duality" of the contents herein is entirely conscious and consistent, and thus I should request that our noteworthy "critics" restrain themselves from rediscovering this particular America.

Lwów, 1923

Ah, and what a leg it was! A leg slightly swollen . . .
> — Dostoevsky, *The Brothers Karamazov*

It will happen one morning, or one afternoon . . .
> — Jasieński, "A Ballad of Trams"

1

When the fourteen pairs of anxious hands, both bare and gloved, finally pulled the blood-stained body of Izolda Morgan from beneath the front platform of tram No. 18, her legs severed horribly below the groin and just hanging on by a few strips of tendon, all those gathered around had the sudden and unpleasant feeling of having committed a faux pas.

The girl was twenty-three, her ample chestnut hair scattered in disarray, her face flawlessly beautiful, and her magnificent, shapely legs reaching up to a pair of almost breast-high hips — the unmistakable sign of a thoroughbred.

After that, everything happened at breakneck speed.

The ambulance came and went, packing the whole incident up inside. An hour later, both legs were amputated, and that evening the patient — having been deposited in a private room of the clinic — fell into a heavy, dreamless, reinvigorating sleep.

2

Berg, off gallivanting that week in another city, was only informed of these events the following day by a vague and curt letter that mentioned an accident of some sort and requested he come at once.

The tumult of the train platform, the slam of the doors, the smell of fresh paint, the galloping kaleidoscope of trees through the diaphragm of the window — like the beads of a rosary threaded on his blunt, hollow anxiety, it all slid into the depths of a long, horizontal crack.

Facing the on-duty doctor, he was quite calm as he listened to the dry, technical report.

After the explanations had concluded, he asked permission to see her.

He entered the private room accompanied by the doctor.

The patient was not asleep.

She was supine, her eyes wide open.

Berg stood by her legs. He had prepared himself to say something, but right at that moment he couldn't quite recall what would be appropriate.

(. . . the heavy, luxuriant candles of chestnut blossoms in that long, ruthless, tunnel-vision perspective, the cool, moist taste of lips against lips, the warmth of a tiny hand through suede gloves . . . Do you remember? . . .)

He even tried to smile, but at that moment his eyes fell upon the sagging line of the blankets that marked the inconceivable void below her hips.

(. . . God, God, just don't think . . .)

A sticky-sweet fluid slid up his larynx.

And again the chestnut blossoms, and again the taste of moist lips, and the long, slender leg emerging from the sunny foam of her skirts.

(. . . shhhh, I'm not going to scream, not now . . .)

What a funny face the doctor had. The left side of his mustache drooped like a cockchafer's, and there was a tiny pimple at the tip of his nose.

Then he saw her eyes, the eyes of a cowering, whipped dog (. . . in his father's yard, they had drowned his puppies . . .), begging for mercy, boring into him with anxious anticipation.

He felt a welling confusion under that gaze, aware that he was blushing like a schoolboy, that he'd been standing there a good few minutes, that it was high time he said something, and that *he wasn't going to say anything at all.*

He suddenly wanted to run away.

(. . . on the street: people, carriages, rumble, trams, trrr . . .)

Why does that doctor's face seem so peculiar? Oh, there's the doorhandle, now he just had to head back home.

He took the stairs four at a time until he made it back onto the street, blending in with the motley, feverish crowds.

He collapsed, overheated, red as a matador's cape. Round, round infinity. And over the distended "i" of the city, the gigantic dot of the sun.

People ran, walked, shoved, cars snarled, trams rang, spitting out and swallowing new cargoes of people at the stops, racing past him with a monotonous grind of their polished rails.

3

Late in the evening a well-dressed young man presented himself to the clinic's senior orderly, Tymoteusz Lerche, an old, stocky cadger with a pockmarked face and ginger stubble. The stranger motioned the orderly to one side, fingering a five-hundred franc bill, and asked him if he would do him a certain favor.

Tymoteusz Lerche assured the stranger that he was entirely at his disposal.

The stranger thus clasped him affectionately by the arm and explained that he was a relative of one Izolda Morgan, a victim of a tram accident who had been brought in two days before, and that — should such a thing prove possible (here the banknote made a telltale rustle) — he sought to obtain his cousin's amputated legs.

Tymoteusz Lerche showed not the slightest sign of surprise, nodding his head obligingly to show he understood, though he wasn't sure if the limbs in question hadn't been thrown out with the trash. Then he went off, indicating that his guest should take a seat.

After twenty minutes he returned with a big, long box under his arm, carefully wrapped in packing paper. The package looked just as if it had come from a fashionable clothing boutique, and the pink ribbon decorating it was a classy touch.

Tymoteusz Lerche handed the package to the stranger in silence. The five-hundred francs vanished into a pocket. He then asked if the stranger would not like a boy to deliver the package to his door.

This the stranger declined. He tucked the package under his arm and left with it on his own, seen off by low bows from the orderly and the two doormen.

4

In the office where Berg was employed the news of his misfortune spread like wildfire, creating a general atmosphere of hushed whispers and silent sympathy.

The City Power Co., where Berg was one of twelve engineers, offered him a month's leave. Berg declined the offer. He kept getting up bright and early for work, just like before. He was never seen in the evenings. The friends who thought to visit him at this time found a note on the door: "Do not disturb."

It was common knowledge that he hadn't been to see Izolda since his visit to the clinic, and this was accounted for in various ways. Otherwise, he behaved quite normally, chitchatting and smiling. Over time, suspicion grew that his love for Izolda had simply not been that strong. This came to be generally accepted. Soon everyone stopped bothering about him. Those around him vaguely resented his having come to terms with the situation and forgetting the incident so easily.

5

The legs were compellingly white and curiously long. They reached their terminus at a tiny, narrow, high-arched foot, satisfactorily slender in the fetlocks, fulsome in the flawlessly modeled shanks, very long, hard, and firm. Small, dainty knees gave way to white thighs with a velvety sheen, covered by a whole network of barely perceptible blue veins, thus lending the woman's body the gravity of marble. Delicate feet still rested in low, patent-leather slippers, and the black silk stockings enfolded the legs above the knees, much like when they supported their owner. The amputation had happened quickly and was, of necessity, directly below the groin, so there had been no point in undressing the legs entirely. Placed on a settee, one leg crossed haphazardly over the other, and with a blanket folded thickly around their thighs, they looked like the animated limbs of a woman covered and sleeping.

Berg sat by them for hours at a time. He knew each and every muscle, and could call them by name. Tracing a hand along the *quadriceps cruris*, his fingers gently stroked the inner thigh, at precisely the spot where the groin is joined to the knee by the slender, hardly perceptible *gracilis* muscle, also known as the *defensor virginitatis*, the weakest of all the female leg muscles. All of his painful love for Izolda was concentrated on her legs. He lay for hours on the settee, his lips nuzzling the soft, fragrant skin of the flushed thighs, just like before, when he had caressed them, back when they had belonged to her. It was rare that he thought of Izolda *as such*. To be precise, he didn't think of her at all. That scene at the clinic had left him with little more than a sense of estrangement and revulsion. Why on earth should he care for that mutilated stump of a woman, that shapeless trunk, hideous and tragic. He cuddled up to her marvelous legs — of which he was now sole proprietor — in sweet exhaustion, feeling entirely at peace.

That Izolda's legs were as pink and fresh after two weeks as they had been the day of the operation seemed in no way unnatural to him. He could not have conceived it differently. It would have seemed equally nonsensical to him had someone claimed that Phidias' Nike was at risk of decay because her head was missing. These were still, after all, the legs of a living woman, severed from the body by a simple accident, but this did not mean they had ceased to be an organic part of her – they were joined forever with the vital oneness of her indivisible personality.

6

Twelve o'clock at night. Berg is working the night shift at the power station. He could in fact just sit in his room up above, but somewhere (deep down) he's afraid of solitude, though he does not allow this thought to overwhelm his consciousness.

The bright light of the lamps and the rhythmic clatter of the machines have a narcotic, lulling effect.

Berg walks up and down between two rows of galloping machines.

The whiz of whirling spokes and the rattle of pivots.

The music of red-hot steel.

He stares for a moment at a spinning wheel and feels a slight vertigo.

A minute later his attention is drawn to a great piston, rising and falling with uniform precision. It makes a hollow, tired, panting sound. Berg is reminded of sexual intercourse. He stares in horror as the gigantic piston indefatigably rises and falls. The machine is copulating. "Why don't they just reproduce," says Berg, and he feels a cold shudder go down his spine. "Wild, sterile beasts," he snarls at them without looking back as he hurries his step.

But he cannot see the end of the walkway. To the right and

the left the pivots are rising and falling at an insane speed. Berg feels a gust of hard, ruthless hatred blowing on him from the machines. The eternal hatred of the worker for his exploiter. He feels tiny and defenseless surrounded by these iron creatures, utterly at their mercy. He wants to scream, but he seizes control of himself with the remnants of his consciousness. "They hate me," he thinks clearly, "but they are bolted down tight and cannot harm me."

As if to prove to himself that he is not afraid, he stops in front of one of the machines and gives it a derisive glare.

Here the gears turn a bit slower, more lazily. The beast is lurking in wait. Berg suddenly feels an ungovernable desire to reach out and touch a spoke. He cannot tear his eyes from the steel of the slide.

"I'll just touch it and pull back at once," he lucidly thinks.

He wants to tear away from it and flee, but he cannot. The wheel seems to spin more and more slowly, more and more lazily . . . Like a giant arm, the spoke reaches further and further outward . . . He can feel its cold breath. In a moment it'll touch his face. Mother of God!

Berg suddenly feels a sharp pain in his arm. Someone's bony hand has tossed him aside with incredible strength. He hears a stern, gravelly voice, like the horn of Jericho:

"Careful! You could've fallen into the machine."

He sees a worker's soot-blackened face looming over him, large blue eyes staring at him from under a furrowed brow.

"Why don't you go upstairs and get some sleep, we can take care of this ourselves," the voice says with that same commanding tone, making Berg feel powerless, weak, and childlike.

The strong bony hand leads him, practically carries him through the hall and releases him in the courtyard.

"Thank you," says Berg softly, and he sees the enormous, black face of the sky above him, pockmarked with stars.

7

A week after this event, Berg left the power station earlier than usual and headed away from town.

The golden autumn day smelled of hibiscus. The infinite calm of the air was disquieting, terrifying. Everything was in slumber, not a branch was stirring. In this dead silence only the leaves fell on the sand, one after another, in long, spiraling serpentines. The motionless poetry of autumn.

> *Dry leaves are falling,*
> *slowly, rhythmically lolling,*
> *rustling, hovering over the earth in fear*
> *of the air, of torpid death.*
> *Over their cartilage bed,*
> *lily, golden, red,*
> *the sun is setting, out of breath,*
> *anemic, melancholy.*

A senior mechanic named Ginter had just fallen into the gears of the largest machine. By the time they managed to extract him, he was reduced to a shapeless pulp. Berg found this recollection rather unpleasant and tried not to think about it.

Since that memorable night the week before, Berg had been conscious of a constant and unrelenting animosity that grew with every passing day, one which he was unable to shake. Whenever he had to walk across the shop floor, he did so very quickly, without glancing to either side. The wind of dull, powerless hatred that blew through the machine hall filled him with a cold and inexpressible terror. He searched the faces of the workers to find evidence of the same feeling, but they were inscrutable, their stares haughty and grim. For some time Berg had been oppressed by the thought that these people had all gone mad from having worked there so many years. He caught himself watching their movements in order to confirm his theory. Whenever he had to exchange a few words with the workers, he could feel himself growing flustered, and would abruptly end the conversation.

"I must keep from going mad myself," Berg thought, and just at that moment, envisioned a plan to change his position.

Yes, that would be for the best. He'd transfer, take an office job. That would definitely calm his nerves.

Suddenly he heard an inhuman whiz from behind him. He was struck by the running board of a car driving past and tossed onto the sidewalk. Obscenities poured out as it went.

This thoroughly disoriented him. He had to lean against a tree to regain his bearings. The fear deep inside crawled out and stared him in the eyes.

"I'll have to think this through, think it through . . ." Berg repeated to himself; yet he felt as though everything had been plotted in advance for him. There was no exit. Only a moment earlier he had thought, in comical naiveté, that all he needed was to change his position to protect himself from the machines' hatred. Now he could see that the machines were lurking everywhere in wait. His every step hinged on the machines.

Berg suddenly felt hemmed in. All the machines he had ever seen came slinking out from the crannies of his consciousness and cinched him in an iron ring. A scream shimmered in him like a faint thread of light in this labyrinth, a name: Izolda!

He looked around. He was somewhere far away, in a strange neighborhood. Only now did he feel his exhaustion. It was time to head home.

A tram was approaching. Berg shuddered at the sight of it. He wanted to scream. He stared into the face of a passenger on the right-hand side. It was kindly, calm and content, like a mask. Suddenly, under the pressure of Berg's gaze, the monstrous crack of a grin split the mask in two, and for a moment Berg saw the red, yawning maw of insanity just inches from his face.

8

The mood in the power station kept getting stranger. Ever since Ginter's tragic death, the imperceptible whispers exchanged between the workers had been building into a soft growl. They were speaking of a strike.

Berg increasingly stumbled across congregations of workers in the machine hall. They dispersed at the sight of him. A small, square-shaped manifesto had been hanging on the power-station door for two days, and no one had torn it down.

That night, Berg wept for a long time, his face pressed against

Izolda's legs. The time had come. Fate was pushing him, casting him in the role of liberator.

9

The machine hall was black and yawned the void. The instant Berg shut the door behind him he stood leaning against a wall, with a steadily diminishing conviction of what had brought him here. He'd been coming since he was a fresh-faced engineer, but he had never seen the hall so silent and dark. He was bewildered. At first he wanted to fire up all the electricity, but then he recalled that there was a blackout across the whole city, because the power station wasn't in operation. Consciousness returned. He tried to sober his thoughts. He pulled a lantern from his pocket and lit it. A sharp beam of light cut through the gloom, making the black void seem even darker. The huge contours of wheels emerged from the darkness like the black wings of giants.

Berg felt that if he had to stay one moment longer he would beat a retreat. He took a few steps. His legs were moving mechanically now. The path was oddly long. Berg thought he'd passed it. He would have to turn back. He raised the light. And only then did he observe that he was standing directly below the control panel. The eyes of two clocks glowed in his bright beam of light.

Berg pulled a hammer and a file from his coat pocket.

The eyes of the clocks drilled into him, cold and sober. The hand grasping the hammer was steady and cool. Now all he needed was presence of mind.

The eyes of the manometers became bizarre and magnetic.

Berg recalled a fakir he'd seen at the circus who paralyzed a snake with his gaze. Now he knew what the snake felt — he had come to sink in his fangs and was unable to move, shackled by this strange gaze. This lasted a while. Then, with his last bit of willpower, Berg suddenly lifted his hammer and, with a strength incomprehensible even to himself, brought it crashing down on the control panel.

The crack of marble shattered the silence.

A calm that was bright, warm, and deep as a pond . . .

And then the inconceivable happened: a bright, infinite light blinded him for a moment. The black, motionless wheels started to turn. Berg felt a hard knock on the head and fell, his face hitting the floor.

10

On page four of the only newspaper that was distributed over the course of the following hour, a small notice printed in brevier appeared amid the other articles:

". . . caught red-handed in an act of sabotage right as he was trying to destroy the machines of the city power station, Engineer Witold Berg will be put before the workers' tribunal . . ."

11

The gigantic empty factory hall was filled with a sea of human heads. A makeshift tribune had been slapped together from a few packing crates. A lean, freckled student with white fluttering eyelashes was reading out the accusation in a monotone. A sleek, dark-haired bookkeeper with a large nose was slowly, gingerly flipping the pages of a ledger. The freckled student raised his voice from time to time; it rang out in a whine, echoing through the murmur of the crowd, like a wind sweeping through the hall.

The hearing stretched on, tedious and futile. Everyone knew the verdict, it was just about going through the formalities.

The student finally sat down, wiping his nose with a handkerchief, and the bookkeeper turned to the right with a nondescript gesture, his voice thin and metallic:

"Please bring in the accused."

A hollow murmur swept through the hall. Then the door on the right opened somewhat too loudly, and Berg walked in, escorted by four workers armed with Mausers. The crowd parted a bit to let him approach the tribune.

The rumble grew, slowly building into a roar of hostile voices.

A bell.

The hearing proceeded.

The hands of the clock moved with the stubborn inertia of a turtle.

Suddenly the noise built, and the crowd of heads turned toward the tribune, as if pushed in that direction. Berg was standing on the tribune.

He was very pale, his eyes twitched, a lock of hair fell onto his face. He was dressed impeccably, wearing a jacket. He spoke in a sonorous, calm voice, often pausing to find the right expression:

"The day of vengeance is upon us. Conscious of its goals, the proletariat is standing up to fight. If the fight is to succeed, we must remind ourselves, above all, who our mortal enemy is. Destroy this enemy, and the evil will be banished. The bourgeoisie is surely an enemy, but they are not our *prime* enemy. Take away the bourgeoisie's money and the proletariat will increase a millionfold. But this would not solve the problems of the proletariat. Our enemy is different, much closer, one the worker faces every day in the factory. It imperceptibly devours his strength, his health, and sometimes even his life. Our enemy is the machine. It is no accident that bourgeois civilization prides itself on the machine as its greatest accomplishment, the source of a million conveniences. But in thinking that the machine has simply given them a new weapon for combating the elements and a new method for exploiting the proletariat, the bourgeoisie are mistaken. The machine has swollen like a parasite, burrowing into all of life's nooks and crannies, slowly transforming from tool to ruler. The bourgeoisie have been utterly conquered by the machine and cannot do without it.

"But the worker has always loathed the machine. It has always been his misery and his curse. Tens of thousands of unemployed, thousands of deaths and mutilations, widows and orphans going hungry — this is the machine for the worker. Now, in this time of open and triumphant combat, the task of the proletariat lies here: to liberate humanity from the machine. We must destroy the machines, destroy them at once, lest they destroy us first."

At that moment Berg was beautiful. His cheeks were flushed and his hair fell over his brow.

There was some applause and a long pregnant silence. Berg stepped down from the tribune.

The freckled student rose from the table. He was frightened. He rapidly blinked his eyes. He spoke in a quick and aggravated voice.

It seemed to him as though the engineer only sought to mock the tribunal, but the applause he heard (he glanced hesitantly to the side) demanded a response. The destruction of the machines, which are the cultural legacy of all of humanity, and thus of the proletariat as well, would be a return to barbarism. The machines serve the masters and the workers alike. How would the proletariat get by without the machines? After all, trams and waterworks are machines as well, and everyone benefits from them.

Berg did not hear him out. He walked through the crowd and into the street. People made way for him. The rain fell fine, autumnal, blurring his eyes like tears. Berg felt like something had him by the throat. His entire speech and appeal had seemed like a comical parody. What sense did it make? They were just like the others, only a bit less "intelligent." And anyway, it was too late.

12

When the general strike erupted a few days later, Berg went out to the street in the morning. The day was bright and sunny. The squares were all silent. There was not a single tram in sight.

Berg chose the widest avenue and walked down it. The streets were undulating strangely, as though inebriated. Unrest peeked out from all the doorways. The silence grew heavy. Everything was crouched low, as if anticipating what was to come. Berg walked faster. The uncanny silence was beginning to tire him. He wanted to return home.

At the street corner someone grabbed him by the arm. He knew those pale blue eyes and peaked cap from somewhere. The mechanic from the power station.

"I heard you speak at the tribunal," he said in a bright, soothing voice. "I didn't understand everything, but you said the time had come for the machines to start ruling us, and not we them. But as you can see, one flick of a finger and everything comes to a halt. Silent as before the world was created. What do you say to that?"

He radiated and exuded sunlight and joy, power: We! We!

Berg stared into his face and was gripped by a maddening urge to tear the joy from him, to see animal terror fill those round eyes.

They walked along the sidewalk toward the triumphal arch. Berg said:

"It's all the same by now. You don't understand the souls of the machines, though you have stood closest to them. But it's so simple. The soul of the machine is motion, *perpetuum mobile*. We, on the other hand, breathe the air of limitations. The consequences are clear. We've given ourselves a lethal injection that will eventually overcome us.

"We're nearing the end with mathematical certainty. Soon everything around us will be replaced by machines. We shall live among machines. Our every move is dependent on machines.

We are laying down our arms. We are putting ourselves entirely in the hands of a foreign, hostile element. Our iron nerves are still straining to hem them in, to maintain our hegemony, but they will burst their bonds, and soon. Then what remains will either be a struggle or madness. For the time being, no one sees or understands this. We are blinded by our own power. There is no escape. We've painted ourselves into a corner. Anyway, it's already inside of us. You cannot move a muscle anymore without machines. Your parents perhaps could still manage. But you no longer can. You cannot defend yourselves. You can only wait. The poison is inside of us. We've poisoned ourselves with our own power. The syphilis of civilization."

"Goodbye!" he said, suddenly bending over to the mechanic's ear, grasping his hand and squeezing it. "I'm going that way . . ."

13

Late one evening, when the on-duty officer at Police Precinct X was just turning in for a quick nap, a cadaverously pale man with shiny eyes appeared at the precinct, introducing himself as Witold Berg, engineer at the city power station, and reported that his legs had been stolen. He demanded to be assigned a few detectives for immediate assistance and insisted there was not a second to lose.

There were only two people at the time at the precinct, and thus the on-duty officer informed him most courteously that he would have to wait a moment as there were no men present and he would have to call for them. The man declared that he could not wait a single second, and if this precinct were unable to provide him help, then he would look for another.

The on-duty officer used all possible arguments to detain him. The officer who had gone to telephone came back and declared that detectives would arrive within three minutes.

They proceeded to draft a report.

They were incapable, however, of extracting from the stranger anything apart from the fact that on the evening in question, when he had been absent from his apartment, his legs had been stolen.

"Here they are," the officer said warmly, "there was no reason to get upset."

Six stocky men entered the room, flanking the door on both sides.

"These men are at your disposal," the officer said. "Please be so kind as to show them the way."

Berg shook the officer's hand, extended with the greatest of enthusiasm, and went out. But he had not made it across the threshold before he felt twelve powerful hands knocking him to the floor. He tried to get away, he shook, bit, grappled with the men on the ground, even managed to break free a few times, but finally collapsed, knocked out and humiliated. He felt he was sliding down a steep incline, then a moment later he felt the breeze of the damp, autumnal air. At last he realized they were stuffing him into a cramped, tightly-sealed box. The lid of the box slammed shut. Berg fell unconscious.

The on-duty officers at Precinct X were clearly not fated to sleep that night. No sooner had the footsteps faded below than the station was informed that at 14 N. Street, a woman named

Izolda Morgan, who had lost both her legs two months before in a tram accident, had poisoned herself with sulfuric acid.

14

When Berg opened his eyes, it was entirely light out. The white, blinding light of the moon fell through the bars of the small window up near the ceiling. The room was small and unfurnished. The cobblestones on the floor sparkled in the shaft of white light.

He stood up feeling light and spry. Only now did he notice his movements were restricted. He effortlessly removed the odd straitjacket from his arms and stuffed it under the bed.

The moon shone bright and monotonous.

"I'll go out to the street," thought Berg and went to the door. But the door had no handle and was locked. He walked slowly over to the wall, effortlessly shoved it to one side, and walked out.

Once on the street, he was consumed by a feverish crowd surging all in one direction. He was pushed along through unfamiliar, wide, brightly-lit streets. The moon shone like a great electric lamp, casting a strong, chill glow.

On a street corner he felt a tiny hand nestle under his arm. He looked around. A slender young girl with a sweet, childlike face and long, dark eyelashes was walking alongside him. They said nothing. The girl turned at the next corner. He obediently followed her, not troubling himself to think where he might be going. They walked this way down a street. When they reached the next, the girl led him into a huge black building, dimly lit with kerosene lamps. He went up some narrow wooden stairs to the second floor. Her key opened the door.

In the cramped, spartan room she sat him on the bed and started to undress. When she took off her shirt, he saw she had tiny, very white, firm breasts, and wide, finely sculpted hips. He recalled that he had not had a woman in two months. He took her greedily, like a starving man takes bread. Her hips were soft and flexible, as if spring-loaded, they rose and fell rhythmically, so that he could remain motionless and let the act proceed on its own. He took her again and again. When he stretched out tired on the pillows, she started to dress. He then realized he had no money. He told her this. She was not upset. She got dressed quickly. She told him she had to go. They went out. After passing through the door, they went their separate ways.

The street Berg walked down was wide and filled with people. Everyone ran fast, as if anxious about something, in a single direction. To avoid being trampled, Berg stepped off the sidewalk and onto the street. He thought of the strange woman he'd had sex with moments before and her inconceivable hips. At once he heard a long, menacing scrape behind him. He looked back. A tram was coming from the rear. It was practically nudging his back. Only then did he realize that he was walking down the middle of white, slippery rails. He started to run as fast as his strength would allow. He could not veer off to the side. He saw all too clearly that if he stepped one foot on the rails he would slip, and the tram would run him over. He ran straight ahead along the tracks, with a speed he himself could hardly conceive, the menacing song of the tram right behind him in pursuit. He tried to scream — to no avail. There had to be a stop somewhere . . . But the stop would not come. Suddenly one loomed in the distance. Berg strained as much as he could. If only he could get there. He did.

But the tram raced past the stop, rushing forward with unfaltering speed. They passed one stop, and then another. Suddenly Berg felt his hair standing on end and his legs refusing to comply. An old, well-worn eight-line poem he once wrote flashed through his brain:

> *It will happen one morning, or one afternoon,*
> *Unexpected and ordinary, like a sudden death,*
> *At all the corner stops, one day very soon,*
> *The trams will fly past, without pausing for breath.*
> *They'll rattle by in hops, jump from rail to rail,*
> *The necks of their transoms will stick out like divers,*
> *The machines huff and flush, their faces turn pale,*
> *The 18s, 16s, and 25ers . . .*

Looking around, he saw the tram touching his back. An 18 glowed on its illuminated face.

Trams drove past. On one of the rear platforms Berg saw Izolda leaning on the guardrail, waving a handkerchief at him.

Then, with a last burst of energy, he grabbed the protruding eyes of the taillights with both hands and hung in the air.

Long, deranged trams flew past one after another, full of pale passengers, their faces mad with terror.

POLISH FUTURISM
(AN ACCOUNTING)

Futurism is a form of collective consciousness that must be overcome. I am no longer a Futurist, but every one of you is a Futurist. A manifesto is a threshold to be crossed. The machine is no product of man; it is his superstructure. The object forms of civilization as the beauty of modern man's body. The story of my Futurism. Down with Futurism.

As a matter of fact, I have already written the history of Futurism. The critics and the reading public overlooked it, because it came packaged as a "novel," and it bore a curious title: *The Legs of Izolda Morgan*. Today I would have written it somewhat differently. It can be hard for the miners who drill tunnels in the rocks of the modern collective consciousness to take in the beauty of the vantage points these same tunnels provide. That is a job for history's idle tourists.

Futurism is a certain brand of collective consciousness. In order to speak of it, we must first conquer it within ourselves. But the struggle that every triumph invariably entails has its own shortsighted and dazzling perspectives, and whatever falls within its field of vision takes on a special illumination. This is why whenever I speak of Futurism, I get the feeling that I am broaching a very private and intimate topic.

In Poland, the word "Futurist" has acquired an unflattering meaning that obscures its original content. It has become a slur.

Tracing this phenomenon would occupy too much of our time.

Our transgression lies entirely in our having seized a certain historical moment in the modern consciousness, one we all share. Instead of denying it, we tried to harness it in new forms of art. Only when these forms have been created can we speak of having conquered the moment itself. Keeping silent takes us not one inch forward – moreover, it eliminates all potential for progressive action. This is the source of many rather comical reversals. The present situation, for example, is the exact reverse of what the public supposes to be true. I am no longer a Futurist, whereas you, ladies and gentlemen, are one and all Futurists. It may seem paradoxical, but there you have it.

Upon returning to Poland in 1918 I first met Tytus Czyżewski. There was one thing we knew for certain:

The roaring swell of modern life had burst the floodgates, the trenches, the barbed wire, and had broken into the sea of the Polish psyche with irresistible force. This life knew no equivalent in the Polish consciousness.

The consciousness of a society is its art, conceived as organized life. Every new phase of life requires new forms in art. It is only through the creation of forms that the contemporary moment enters the collective consciousness, becoming an organic moment – and thus a creative one. On the other hand, a society that cannot create new forms of organization in time is overthrown, conquered, colonized by the moment of modern life it is incapable of harnessing.

The massive and rapid growth of forms in technology and industry is undoubtedly the foundation and the backbone of the contemporary moment. It has created a new ethic, a new esthetic, a new reality. The introduction of the machine as an indispensable and complementary component in man's life was necessarily accompanied by a fundamental reconstruction of his psyche, by the creation of new correctives, much like the introduction of a foreign substance into a living organism forces it to secrete specific antibodies; these turn antigens into substances that can be either assimilated or expelled. If the human or social organism does not manufacture this energy in the requisite quantities, the foreign substance begins to contaminate or to poison.[1]

Manufacturing these mental antibodies — that is, creating forms to subordinate the machine to mankind — is the present task of modern art.

The moment this truth became conscious, Futurism was born.

Italian Futurism responded to it long before the war, and Russian Futurism shortly thereafter — though in polar opposite fashion.

The response of Italian Futurism was simple, and it can be summed up in a single sentence:

Art should elevate the machine to become the erotic ideal of humanity.

(A position defended long, hard, and persistently in Poland by one Tytus Czyżewski, a great artist.)[2]

But to adore is not to overcome — on the contrary, it entails

---

[1] In *The Legs of Izolda Morgan* I demonstrated the process whereby the machine infected the contemporary psyche.

[2] "Love thee the electric machines, wed with them and bear Dynamo-children — magnetize and shape them, so that they may grow to be mechanized citizens" ("1st Futurist Pamphlet," June 1921).

submission to the object of adoration. This commonly occurs in a consciousness at its lowest rung of development, and is one of the most primitive forms of response to external phenomena.

Primitive man worshipped the elements because he felt entirely defenseless against them. At a higher stage of development, this relationship changed into one of revolt to vanquish the unknown quantity, only to settle thereafter into a self-confident power following this overthrow.

The response of Russian Futurism was double-edged from the very beginning:

> Things are your enemy —
> Get that into your head.
> Things should be crushed!
> Or maybe loved, instead?
> Or maybe they have souls unlike ours? . . .[3]

All of Russian Futurism from 1913 to 1919 is an oscillation between these two truths, bouncing from one to the other. It was only Mayakovsky's *Mysterium Buffo* of 1919 that voiced the final response of Russian Futurism:

> Comrade Things,
> Tell you what —
> Let's make a truce, as it's said.
> How about this: we'll make you,
> And you shall keep us fed.

[3] Mayakovsky, *Vladimir Mayakovsky, a Tragedy*, 1913.

This response, drawn from socialism, designates a place for the machine in the modern consciousness not unlike the one that capitalist society designates for the worker.

Polish art, rousing itself from its national-patriotic lethargy after the war, had a ready, though misleading, response in Italian Futurism. This had to be scrutinized and either accepted or discarded — and if it were to be discarded, there had to be another response to put in its place.

The moment postwar Polish thought and European thought crossed swords, Polish Futurism was born.

It was born at a strange and singular time.

The gates to the West were suddenly flung open before a Polish mind that had been soaking in a four-year bloodbath. Having been preoccupied with its own national issues, it had never directly taken part in the riddle of contemporary European culture; now a solution was expected.

The virus of modernity descended upon the Polish organism before it could be vaccinated. A fight between the organism and the virus broke out, a life and death struggle, a hasty, wild manufacture of local antitoxins. The Polish organism fell into a crisis and flailed in a feverish state. The fever produced in the Polish organism by the virus of modernity, this period of struggle, and the organism's painful transformation will go down in the history of modern culture under the heading *Polish Futurism*.

From the outside, this simply looked like a war a particular group of artists had declared on their society. This "society" boarded itself up in the bastions of its churches and editorial offices, from which it poured buckets of filthy, corrosive water onto the partisans, shouted down their poetry evenings, and showered them with eggs and stones. Nobody was really too clear on why the battle was being waged and what its actual significance was. The Polish psyche felt its traditional customs and dependencies were being undermined, and it defended them with a vigor that could hardly have been anticipated.

The initial critiques — exemplified by the press — made every effort to belittle the process, presenting it as no more than a "trend" imported from abroad. They even spewed up a whole generation of fishermen with academic rods and reels to hook gudgeons from the stormy waters of echoes and delusional plagiarisms. These fish they triumphantly carried before the public to prove that the process they found so disturbing was in no way domestic, that it was little more than an effort to foist some strange "foreign" ideas upon them.

The public had its doubts.

Then the critics changed their approach. They sounded the alarm. They began conjuring up the evil specter of Bolshevism and an anonymous great power. Governmental repression ensued.

Confiscated books and journals, policemen obstructing and dispersing literary evenings, officials expelling artists from various provinces — all these facts, utterly incomprehensible to the foreign artist and only serving to sow rumors of "Polish barbarism" abroad, were simply further stages of the very same struggle.

I recall one of our first sizable evenings at the Warsaw Philharmonic on February 9, 1921, attended by over 2,000 people, crammed into the aisles and crowded around the stage. One audience member came with a snake, a woman brought a monkey. This was how Warsaw demonstrated that it was futurizing.

We recited poems. People stood on their chairs and tried to shout us down. The poems were bad, but the audience didn't seem to notice. I remember Irena Solska, an actress of exceptional courage and brilliant intuition, giving some of her most beautiful renditions to a lifeless response, apart from the hostile murmur of idiots.

In another instance, the same audience wanted to lynch the poet Aleksander Wat as he recited his *namopaniki* – epic poems whose words had been liberated from the yoke of logical content.

These days, when there is far less screaming at my poetry readings (apart from that of the police, a conservative institution by its very nature, who will surely have difficulty forsaking their tried-and-true methods for some time to come), when our books are selling in increasing numbers and have even (!) found more sponsors, when our artistic output is gradually becoming a handbag rummaged through by even those artists who adamantly reject any kind of relationship with us,

these days, when the crisis can be considered a thing of the past, though the process itself is in no way over,

we might cast a calm eye back to the last five years and work out a kind of summation.

We wrote a lot of bad poems, produced a lot of bad paintings – history will forgive us.

It was a strange and beautiful time, a time where every strophe was a thrust, every poem a parry, when poetry was cooked up like dynamite, every word a primer cap, a time of eternal vigilance and constant alert, of straining the eyes to locate the soft spots for striking a blow.

And these days, when I write bad poetry less frequently, I look back on those feverish years, full of intuition and unspoken words, those virginal years of budding values, with something like real regret.

For the "jubilee enthusiasts"[4] — a few dates.

It began slowly, sometimes foretold by an odd and uncanny echo, like thunder before a storm.

Right before the war, in 1914, the tragic herald and John the Baptist of Polish Futurism, Jerzy Jankowski (author of *Tram Athwart the Streat*), had terrified the Polish public with his poems in assorted journals — he was the first Polish Futurist in the Italian sense of the term. These poems vanished without a ripple. The book came out too late. Illness struck him from the ranks of the frontrunners before he was able to take his place.[5] And although Jankowski did not turn the tides of the popular movement, he will always remain a symbol in our literature of the new, rebirthing Polish psyche, as the first herald of new days, when

> the bloody gleam triumphed over water
> the salvo of machine guns, the dry quake
> rang in the aisle of the old temple
> for Futurism's daybreak.[6]

---

[4] An expression borrowed from Mayakovsky, a Russian Futurist.

[5] In 1921, Jankowski (1887–1941) was afflicted with a mental illness that was to plague him till the end of his life. [Tr.]

[6] A not entirely accurate quotation of the last stanza from Jankowski's "Tram Athwart the Streat." [Tr.]

Simultaneously, in the other capital of Poland – Krakow – a lone great artist, Tytus Czyżewski, was shut up in his secluded studio percolating increasingly peculiar and enigmatic forms in the crucible of his intuition.

When I returned to Poland after an extended leave, I found him surrounded by a group of painters who were known outside of Krakow as the Formists. They were just beginning to publish a tiny journal edited by Leon Chwistek and Czyżewski, named after their group. The Formists struck me as a kind of medieval guild in search of new forms. Fenced off from the street by the glass panes of their studios, they solved painting problems one after another just as you would mathematical equations, with iron determination and confidence in their truths. Polish life was surging past on the street outside, sweeping along in a postwar fever, smashing its head against a wall, exhausted in the labyrinths of blind alleys, a tangled sort of life, motley and dumb. It was too late for preliminary work. The moment demanded radical action.

I then met with Stanisław Młodożeniec for the first time, a fresh-faced and promising artist from whom we all expected great things (I don't know why he hasn't been publishing lately).

Thus the first Polish Futurist organization, "Katarynka" (Hurdy-gurdy), was formed. The name was neither as whimsical nor as accidental as it might at first seem. It captured a certain decisive moment for Polish Futurism, a moment when the new Polish art took to the street and the first act of the struggle got underway.

Posters followed in mass quantities, and after the posters – readings.

The fact that the first city to undergo the crisis of Futurism was Krakow, the mausoleum city, Krakow, where every brick is a part of Wawel Castle and every resident a custodian, Krakow the Polish Florence, a waxworks of national mummies — was a perfectly healthy sign, one that bore testimony to the vitality of the Polish organism.

The Polish bourgeoisie had yet to be attacked in its own lair — in Warsaw. The four great readings that subsequently occurred in succession, preceded by the monster reading at the Philharmonic, carried out this task.

In February 1921, Warsaw was stricken.

I first met Anatol Stern and Aleksander Wat in Warsaw. The first manifesto I came across by them, entitled *Yes*, still swathed in the spirit of German Expressionism and prophesying a great coming, was totally alien to me. *Gga* was an almanac published during the course of the Warsaw readings, and promoted Primitivism as a Polish Futurist response. It was an anachronism. Fortunately, their poetry was a far cry from their "Primitivist" manifesto.

After long discussions, a united front of Polish Futurism was formed in Warsaw. The first show of this was the readings held in Łódź in March 1921, which resulted in the "1st Futurist Pamphlet," *Manifestoes of Polish Futurism* (Krakow, June 1921), scattered through all the cities of Poland by the thousands.

In the *Manifestoes of Polish Futurism* I brought together a number of ideas that we were grappling with and were particularly timely. The *Manifestoes* did not represent a program that had been deliberated on and sanctioned by a Congress of Polish Futurists. The ball was rolling. The public required an ideological passport from us, and they were fully entitled to it. I sketched out the most general propositions in these texts, allowing us all under its wing without having to resort to any individual amputations.

The *Manifestoes* first gave Polish Futurism a clear face, drawing bold lines between it and the Futurisms of Italy and Russia, despite certain undeniable correspondences. Let the future historians of Futurism research where these connections lie. I myself do not possess even the most basic requisites for the task. As I have said, Futurism is an intimate affair for me. Every day that is consciously lived turns into dead matter, for which I have nothing but contempt. I am the whole of the present day. I do not understand the past. It suffers from the lack of a "now." Every "yesterday" taken independently loses all meaning. It only regains significance through every new "today." The *Manifestoes* were aware of this when they advocated timely works of art that have a 24-hour life span.

The *Manifestoes of Polish Futurism* are a formulation of what was, in premise, no more than organic ferment.

To be sure, the end of every movement is spelled by its manifesto. The process is the exact reverse of what the public supposes. It scarcely matters if, sometimes for many years after announcing its faith, a given group behaves as though it is fulfilling the declared mission. This is a common delusion. Once a movement has been captured in a statement it is a dead movement, a threshold to be crossed. It is people who are alive – those who do not limit themselves to their own manifestoes. This has nothing to do with the haphazardness (which I consider equivalent to thoughtlessness) and rejection of everything in art that smacks of a "program" currently rampant in Poland. He who has never had a manifesto, who has never rejected anything, has nothing to say in life.

The *Manifestoes of Polish Futurism* was its finale. Its swan song was *Nife in the Gutt*, European Futurism's most beautiful broadsheet.

The collective response of Polish Futurism was invented. At that moment it drew to an end.

Everything that comes after has sought and moved toward individual responses.

What was the response of Polish Futurism?

A vast sea of new object forms in civilization spread before the thoroughly Romantic Polish psyche, though it had not had the slightest direct input into making them. It began to enter a certain kind of relationship with these forms. It had to expediently create some forms on its own, which would allow it to adopt this legacy of machine civilization, not as a kind of dead weight, but as its own internal product – in other words, to create forms to subordinate machines to the Polish psyche.

Italian Futurism taught the psyche to see the machine as a corporeal model and ideal. Through constant apotheosis, the Italian Futurists sought to introduce the machine into mass consciousness as an erotic moment.

Russian Futurism conceived of the machine as a product of and a servant to mankind. It reduced the man/machine relationship to a purely economic one, of the employer to the worker.

The response of Polish Futurism was fundamentally different:

With their endless outward expansion, humans have had to manufacture ever-new forms of perception, i.e., they have had to continually reconstruct themselves to adapt to the new exigencies taking shape before them, which they need to confront. One of these forms is the machine. The machine is no product of mankind — it is his superstructure, his new organ, indispensable at this present stage of development. Man's relationship to the machine is the relationship of the body to a new organ. The machine is a slave to mankind only to the same extent that one's own hand can be called a slave, as subject to the commands of the same switchboard of the brain. Removing one or the other would render contemporary man a cripple.

The task of contemporary art is to bring this central moment for the modern conception of culture to the collective consciousness, to turn it into its blood and intuitive sensibility. But art cannot achieve this by extolling the beauty of the machine (a theme no more worthy than a thousand others), nor by incorporating the actual machine into itself (though this might be one of its many methods) — it must be accomplished by art constructing new bodies of its own on the basis of mechanical laws: economy, purpose, dynamics. And thus, in spite of the fact that few Polish Futurists wrote about machines (Jasieński, Czyżewski) compared to the Italians, they achieved incomparably more along the way.

Polish Futurism's achievement is in having taught us to see contemporary man in all his depth, and in having created art for this new man. And this is the basis of the parallel between Futurism and the Renaissance, a parallel that clearly and naturally suggests itself.

The Renaissance first taught man to see the beauty of his own body. It elevated the human body from "matter" — a sheath for the immaterial "spirit" — to a coordinate organ.

Ever since, in man's endless struggle for survival, he has nurtured and manufactured countless organs, which have smothered the world like a polyp's tentacles.

Polish Futurism taught contemporary man to see the beauty of his own enhanced body in the object forms of civilization. It cured him of the fetishism that had plagued contemporary Futurist thought.

This is the key to its enduring value.

Some might complain that I am trying to warp Polish Futurism to fit my own theories, and that the work of my associates does not support the views presented above. This would be a misunderstanding. Futurism is not a school, it is a particular state of consciousness, a mental state through which every conscious individual must today pass before conquering it. There is but one struggle, yet a great many paths and outcomes. I have not written the history of Futurism, I have written the history of *my* Futurism. The fact that I happened to stand for some time at the forefront of the movement that called itself Polish Futurism gives my words a certain objective significance.

Be that as it may, the line I have marked out here can be more or less clearly traced through the work of all the Polish Futurists, and it is to an extent the intuitive air their poetry breathes.

"Song of Hunger" (as, with certain exceptions, all of my work to date) is an attempt to "humanize" the modern city.

The concrete and steel constructions of Tytus Czyżewski (*Green Eye, Night–Day*) were forged in the same fire of pained, limitless self-awareness.

Aleksander Wat's *namopaniki* – poetry broken down into the basic components of words – are an echo of the same struggle with the object, transferred to the linguistic realm, that is, the struggle to divest the object of its autonomous content.

The deformed words of Młodożeniec's poetry speak of the same thing.

And finally, Anatol Stern's theory of nonsense was forged in the fire's hot breath. The noose tightening around man through the growth of object forms in modern civilization, inevitably leading to the total mechanization of the life of the individual who is unable to see it merely as his own perfected organs, forces us to seek an exit. Stern's exit was art. For the human infected by machines, an art based on nonsense might serve as an oxygen tank that allows him to tear free from the ghetto of logic and construction, to find an outlet and a moment's respite. I do not share this view. Nonsense is dynamite. It could become the material for bringing (intellectual) anarchy to the masses. In our era, when the collective is still in session, there is no place for it. As a theorist, Stern represents a serious faction of Futurist thought (stretching from Apollinaire to Dada) that should be duly acknowledged in any history of the movement.

In our day, when we can look back at this period of collective struggle for new forms as having concluded, the distinctions between the various artists are so stark that, in hindsight, one might ask if Polish Futurism ever really existed as a unified whole, or if it was not simply an association of people joined by a shared urge for expansion, all of whom are now finding their true roads. This notion is a common delusion that arises from a lack of historical perspective.

There was a city of Polish consciousness, and there were a handful of partisans who sought to take it by storm.

They were like a mob gathering in a public square to test their strength, arm themselves, and draw up a plan.

And the square was named: Polish Futurism.

And now they have dispersed into the city — each down his own road.

For a single idea — for victory.

Each down his own road.

The city of Polish consciousness is dark and foreboding. It has many side streets, cul-de-sacs, and blind alleys.

Those who don't know it stumble blindly.

The city shut its walls behind them.

There were no streetlamps to guide them.

They struck out into the night.

Each down his own road.

Krakow, September 3, 1923

KEYS
("Potestas Clavium")

And I say also unto thee, that thou art Peter, and upon this rock I will build my church; and the gates of hell shall not prevail against it. And I will give unto thee the keys of the kingdom of heaven: and whatsoever thou shalt bind on earth shall be bound in heaven: and whatsoever thou shalt loose on earth shall be loosed in heaven.

— Matthew 16

... For if ye forgive men their trespasses, your heavenly Father will also forgive you ...

— Matthew 6

1

The crucifix was old and weather-beaten. Perhaps six hundred years old, it was said.

It hung in a niche by the vestibule entrance.

Its wood had hardened and petrified with age, so that its origins could no longer be determined; it stood slightly taller than a man.

It depicted a blackened and withered Christ, fastened to the cross with three massive hobnails.

But the most fascinating thing was Christ's face — it in no way resembled those pious faces the Renaissance painters gave him on their canvases. It was the face of a thug, horridly ugly, with black, sunken eye sockets, a terrible, loathsome expression etched onto his ample, bestial jaws, a face that smacked more of blasphemy than sainthood.

The monk who sculpted it must have been possessed, or a dreadful sinner; he had carved the base evil of his spidery soul.

The legs, half worn to nothing from the kisses of pious lips, were stiff and bony, like the legs of a corpse.

2

The priest felt a strange antipathy toward the crucifix.

Ever since he had first set foot in the parish, at only thirty years of age, he had nursed an incomprehensible, superstitious dread, a hatred for it, which had only grown as the years went by.

Whenever he had to walk past the niche to conduct Mass, he always crossed himself rapidly and hurried on.

He had been here for twenty years, living off the church and the village. When offered a promotion to a better parish he declined. Only his relationship to the crucifix in the vestibule had remained constant since the day of his arrival.

He was not liked by his parishioners.

They knew about his various dealings, and whispered about them in private.

Everyone knew he had fathered two children, a boy and a girl, with his housekeeper, who had died the previous fall. The children were being educated in the city.

He was stern and dogmatic with the villagers.

Miserly and penny-pinching, he begrudged everyone, whether rich or indigent.

He knew perfectly well the parishioners detested him, and this made him all the more ruthless.

A wiry consumptive with broad shoulders and a sunken rib cage, he was still trim despite his fifty years of age. He was silent and glum, his face gaunt and ashen, his eyes blazing but deeply sunken; he gave the impression of a man wracked by illness.

And curiously – though no one seemed to notice it – that

bony, angular face with its phosphorescent eyes resembled that of the Christ in the vestibule.

Had the priest noticed the resemblance? Was this why he resented the crucifix?

Apparently not.

He had been overexerting himself the past few years. That autumn was more difficult and more miserable than the ones before.

Rain fell incessantly, the air was foggy and damp.

He never tended to his illness. He had lived with it for so many years that it had become a part of him.

And one day it happened that, while celebrating Mass, his singing gave way to a terrible fit, coughing up blood.

He toppled from the pedestal, dropping his chalice.

He was carried to the presbytery.

The fit persisted.

By the time the doctor from a nearby town had managed to stanch the hemorrhage, the priest was utterly spent.

He lay supine, yellow as a chasuble, gasping for breath.

The doctor prescribed some powders for him, told him to remain in bed, not to go outside for the love of God, and when the rain let up — to travel.

Gries — Davos — Zakopane . . .

He took his pay and left.

The priest spent two days bedridden.

On the third day he rose and went to conduct Mass, in the morning, as usual.

He was looking much the worse for wear.

He was hobbling with a cane and coughing loudly.

His face was even more sunken and sallow.

He looked like a ghoul.

Thus passed several weeks . . .

3

One night, as the rain was streaming down, a peasant hammered on the doors to the presbytery.

He had come to fetch the priest for his wife, lying in childbirth.

The woman was dying.

The priest cursed loudly, but dressed himself and went.

The rain fell cold and relentless.

The village was far.

The journey left them soaked to the bone.

He was ushered into a clean, well-furnished room.

The woman was fading fast.

Seeing the priest, she propped herself on the pillows and fell into his arms.

The confession began:

"The baby I borne ain't his, ain't my husband's," the woman howled.

"Confess to your husband," the priest commanded.

"God's sake . . . he won't stand for it . . . he'll hurt the kids and himself in the bargain . . . he's so headstrong . . . for God's sake," wailed the woman.

"Send in the husband," ordered the priest.

In came the pale, brawny peasant, who stood at the bedside.

"Speak," the priest commanded.

The woman propped herself up on the pillows.

"Waluś," she howled, "I'm goin' to the Pearly Gates. God Himself's gonna pronounce judgment on me, so I'll tell you everything, just like it's a holy confession."

She stammered a bit to catch her breath, then started speaking, swiftly and clearly.

"The child I borne ain't yours, it's Wicek Szymczak's. Waluś, forgive me, I'm goin' to the Pearly Gates . . ."

"Baśka ain't yours neither, she's the squire's. Waluś, remember, they're orphans. You couldn't give me no children, so I done you no harm . . ."

The peasant went white as the ceiling, but remained silent.

The priest gave the sacrament.

The woman began to die.

4

Upon returning home, the priest coughed blood, a fit even more protracted than the first.

The doctor was sent for; he gave the priest a gelatin injection.

He spoke emphatically, forbidding the priest to leave his bed, and prescribed ice and powders.

Upon leaving, he added:

"Right now is not a good time to travel to the mountains. Better wait till spring."

The priest understood.

He remained silent.

He lay there motionless for two days. On the third day he rose, like the time before, and went to conduct Mass.

He then found out, by chance, that the woman he had visited during the night had died, and the peasant had flown into a fit of jealousy. That night he slaughtered both his children with an ax and then hung himself from the rafters in the barn.

From that morning on, the priest looked increasingly worn and withdrawn.

He stopped hearing confessions, using his illness as an excuse.

He only continued to conduct Mass, as he had before.

His eye sockets sank deeper still, and his jaw jutted forward, the skin a taut sheath.

The people who came upon him crossed themselves superstitiously, their gazes lingering after him.

The villagers said the priest wouldn't make it to winter, something was gnawing at his dying conscience.

The rain continued to fall, incessant, torrential.

5

One night much like the one before, a peasant came to the presbytery, calling for the priest. A woman was dying in childbirth.

He opened the door himself and stood there staring at the peasant, wide-eyed, until the latter asked if the priest wasn't feeling under the weather.

Then fearing that the priest would refuse to come, he wailed that a woman was dying.

She would die without a priest.

They're good horses, ain't far.

The priest kept a long silence. Then he replied: "Wait!" and vanished into the depths of the presbytery.

6

All year long, a small oil lamp had burned before the Christ in the niche.

When the priest entered the vestibule it was almost pitch dark, only a narrow shaft of light from the lamp broke the gloom, flaring up and dimming.

Rain poured outside, drumming on the tin of the church. A sharp, chill wind rang in the glass and rattled the doors.

The priest fell prostrate and lay there in silence, then he got to his knees, paler still, and began to speak:

"I would never ask you for myself, Lord, though I have felt ill at times. You saw this, and you remember.

"I have lived as a dog, and so too I shall die.

"Mea culpa! Mea culpa! Mea maxima culpa!

"A woman is dying without a priest, waiting for the word of God.

"How could I absolve her of her sins when I myself am so filled with sin and guilt!

"I have robbed the parishioners.

"The wretched found no sanctuary in my home.

"I wronged widows and orphans.

"I peddled the word of God.

"Mea culpa! Mea culpa! Mea maxima culpa!"

The wind thrashed at the windows and broke onto the gate, rain pounded the roof.

"I fathered the housekeeper's children.

"I stole from the church funds," the priest spluttered.

"I have two orphans and a father on my conscience. How could I absolve that dying woman?

"Lord, my eyes do not deserve to see the miracle I ask of you, but a woman is dying, she awaits your word.

"Lord, take my coat and go!"

He smashed his head on the floor until the tiles groaned, and lay there a long time, motionless, his head slumped downward.

When he raised it, his mouth was filled with blood.

Christ hung motionless, his head slightly tilted to one side, stony and silent.

"Lord, You have placed an insurmountable burden on your servant's shoulders.

"You see, I have fallen.

"I am a man — how can I resolve what is human?

"Lord take from me the mercy you have given us.

"Scripture says: Render unto God what is God's.

"I am a man, and I cannot endure it."

He tumbled once more to the floor and lay there still and silent.

The blood began to soak his mouth and his nose.

When he rose, he was smeared with blood and terrible to behold.

"You will not?!" he bellowed.

"You seek to redeem the world with the torments of one physical death?

"You have given us keys that you yourself refuse to carry, and ask us to carry them for you?!

"I don't want your keys!

"Here, I return them to you!"

He started tearing his cassock from his body and tossing it in a heap at the foot of the crucifix until he stood there utterly naked, frail, proud.

"For having been so heartless to a man awaiting the word of God, letting me croak like a dog, I, a worm, take your suffering upon me; you go and carry my cross."

He approached the sacristy naked and returned a moment later, carrying a hammer, nails, and tongs.

Then he climbed on the ledge of the niche, took the tongs, and began tearing out the hobnails that held Christ in place.

The nails were old; they had grown into the wood and would not come free.

He struggled with them at length. The blood poured from his mouth and formed a large black puddle on the floor.

At last they gave.

When he had removed the third, he took down the Christ and placed it on the ground.

It was heavy, as if made of lead. Splinters bloodied his hands.

Then he raised the hammer and the nails, crawled once more into the niche, and, putting his left hand where Christ's had been, held up a nail, gripping it with bloody fingers, and struck with the hammer.

He writhed in pain, but he hammered again and again, until the head of the nail sunk into the wrist.

Blood suddenly poured from his mouth, and he hung from the nailed hand, gasping and bruised . . .

7

When the peasant waiting outside became anxious and began knocking once more at the presbytery, he saw the priest leaving the church with a cowl pulled down over his eyes.

He helped him into the cart.

The rain was coming down hard.

It took awhile to reach the woman in labor after all.

When they arrived, it was well past midnight.

The woman was dying on a bed in the room.

She was breathing heavily and struggling to draw in air.

The priest had to bend down to her lips to hear her.

"Last fall . . . Wicek — my husband . . . came back from the army . . . I had a child with Józek . . . we made love . . . there . . . behind the barn . . . with Józek . . . he took an ax . . . aaah! . . . ," the woman wailed.

"Do you repent your sin?" the priest asked.

"Well, now . . . I knows it's a sin . . . to kill a husband . . . sure . . . but I got no regrets . . . He beat me . . . real hard . . . never a kind word . . ."

"If you have no contrition, woman, then what is your sin? Go in peace."

The woman stared at the priest in astonishment.

A moment later she began to howl.

"What's that? . . . No absolution? . . . eternal damnation? . . .

Oh Jesus! . . . Have mercy! . . . he beat me . . . I ain't the guilty one . . . Oh Jesus! . . ."

"I tell you, woman, what is this sin of yours if you have nothing to repent? Go in peace."

But the woman clung to the priest's hand and stared at him in terror.

". . . I'm gonna be judged . . . No absolution? . . . I'm a Christian woman . . . Absolve me! . . . can't you see I'm dying . . ."

The door flew open and a pale, handsome peasant with shifty eyes walked in.

He had clearly been eavesdropping through the door jamb.

"She ain't the guilty one here, it's me," he said, approaching the priest. "You won't absolve a dying woman? Look . . . she's on her way out . . ."

"I tell you, people, what sins are these that you have no repentance? Go with the Lord."

The peasant went up to the priest and grabbed him by the shoulders, but at that moment he fell in a heap, as if struck by lightning.

The priest left.

"Oh lord . . . no absolution . . . oh lord," – and the woman died.

8

When a beggar came to the church the following day to light candles, he ran out with a terrible cry and tore off toward the village, waving his arms.

There was no getting anything out of him.

He just kept shouting crazily and waving his arms toward the church.

A small group gathered and followed after him.

In the vestibule, on the cross in the niche, instead of the Christ, the priest was nailed by one hand, totally naked, bruised, convulsed.

Stalactites of coagulated blood hung from his mouth, forming puddles on the floor.

On the ground next to the cross: a hammer, nails, and tongs.

The wooden Christ was never found.

1925

THE NOSE

But what is the oddest, the most incomprehensible of all is the fact that the authors can choose similar subjects like this. And yet, when you think it over, there is something to it. Whatever anyone says, events like this do occur in this world — rarely, but they occur.

— Nikolai Gogol

Doctor Otto Kallenbruck, a professor of Eugenics, comparative race studies, and racial psychology, an active member of the German Anthropological Society and the German Society of Racial Hygiene, a founding member of the Society for the Enhancement of the German Race, the author of widely discussed books on the application of sterilization, the racial roots of social proletarian pathology among a series of other titles, was sitting in his study at Lichtenstein Allee No. 18, drinking his after-lunch coffee and attentively studying the proofs of his latest book, *The Endogenic Minus Variants of Jewry*. The book, which had appeared only a month earlier, had sold out in the course of a single week, having generated a considerable number of flattering reviews. In view of the overwhelming demand, it had quickly been reissued in a rather large print run.

The said Professor Kallenbruck had grounds, however, to be not entirely satisfied with this manifestation of outward success. Within leading Party circles the book, though meeting with approval, had not escaped criticism. Dr. Gross, the head of the Party's racial policy board, had openly criticized a series of the arguments in Kallenbruck's book for their excessive frankness.

Doctor Gross's opinion was not in the end the decisive one. Yet the Führer himself, snowed under with matters of state, had still not managed to read the book. In the very imperial Ministry of National Education and Propaganda, they had agreed to recommend it as a course book on race studies for secondary schools under the condition that certain corrections were introduced into the new edition.

Professor Kallenbruck was a man of his own conviction, and the new trends in German race studies that had of late taken on an almost official hue following the example of Doctor Gross and his brother-in-arms, Professor Günther, could not but arouse in him total repulsion.

And this was no joking matter! These gentlemen had attempted to refute all the anthropological criteria for the definition of the Nordic race, replacing them with criteria of a purely spiritual order!

According to Professor Günther, it was not the shape of the skull nor the color of hair that decided anything — it was the Nordic spirit and the Nordic frame of mind. "The erect bearing of a soldier and gymnast, chest out, stomach in" that was what, according to Günther, "constituted the essential indication of the Nordic race."[1]

Doctor Gross had gone even further in his latest articles, and stated that in claiming unequivocally that racial diagnosis was upon the basis of external characteristics, Kallenbruck was frightening off the masses and had created a bad impression abroad.[2] Quite recently, in the journal *Völkischer Beobachter*, he had agreed to recognize the equality of different racial substances, bringing to naught the leading role of the Nordic race.

So why then did Messrs. Gross and Günther not go one step

[1] Hans Günther, Ph.D. "Rassenkunde des deutschen Volkes."
[2] Gross. "Ein Jahr rassenpolitische Erziehung." "National-sozialistische Monatshefte." Wissenschaftliche Zeitschrift der NSDAP. Herausg. von Adolf Hitler. Heft 54. 1934.

further and agree with Boas, who had proved that on the basis of a series of anthropological features the Caucasian was more primitive than the Negro, or with Hart, who had refuted any spiritual racial differentiations?!

No, Professor Kallenbruck was proud of his frankness, and on such a fundamental question he was not prepared to make any concessions whatsoever. He would go to the Führer himself and graphically present him with the disastrous state that existed in German racial studies.

Yet by far the most important was that Professor Kallenbruck himself, if he was to place his hand on his heart, was not completely satisfied with his latest book. This was in light of the richer material that he had managed to gather during the course of his two-month research trip around the concentration camps of Germany for his latest paper "On the Favorable Influence of Sterilization on the Mental Abilities of Schizophrenics and Associated Invalids."

Certain parts of his latest book appeared to him to be somewhat inconclusive. Here the professor was thinking specifically about a series of paragraphs from the chapter on the distinctive characteristics of the Semitic nose, as one of the clearly expressed racial minus-variants, and the influence of the form of the nose on the mental profile of Jewry.

Neither Gobineau, nor Ammon, nor Lapuge, nor even G. St. Chamberlain, nor any of the contemporary racial researchers had hit upon such an original idea. It was the research results of a series of German and English laryngologists that had suggested it to Professor Kallenbruck. Based on research conducted on many thousands of school children, they had proved the indisputable influence of the pathological deformations of the nasal cavity on the mental capabilities of teenagers.

The Semitic nose, in comparison to the ideal straightness of the Greco-Nordic nose — and here there could be absolutely no doubt — represented a clear form of pathological deformation. With the passing of the ages it had lost its subjective pathological character and had transformed itself into a typical genetically conditioned racial feature. The influence of this deformation on the folds of the brain and the psychological peculiarities of Jewry was a fact that was totally obvious and in no way required separate evidence.

To date, the irreproachable logic of the conclusions raised no doubts whatsoever. Difficulties arose only later when there had been devised a more detailed classification of the diversities of a prominent and hooked nose as opposed to the straight type so peculiar to the Greco-Nordic race.

It was quite possible, without much effort, to explain the distinct crookedness of the nose characteristic of the French Bourbon dynasty, found widespread to this very day amongst the French aristocracy, by the historical influence of Jewry on French politics and on the entire French nation — so questionable they have been with regard to the purity of their gene pool.

Far more complex was the question of the Roman nose and its characteristic arch.

The Roman nose was an undoubted deviation from the classic straightness of the Greco-Nordic nose. Yet to explain this by means of the involvement of Romans with Jewry would be highly awkward from the political point of view and, perhaps, rash from the scientific one as well.

The lyrical description of the masculine beauty of the Roman nose in contradistinction to the coarse thickness and deformity of the Semitic nose also failed to satisfy the inquisitive and demanding intellect of Professor Kallenbruck, an intellect accustomed to rigorous academic typologies. Epithets like "sculptured" or "aquiline" were criteria derived more from the field of aesthetics than anthropology.

This weak link in his book, which in its entirety was a startling achievement, had cost the professor many a sleepless night, both before and after its publication.

The new, increasingly flexible border between the Greco-Nordic and the Semitic types of nose that he had taken on board as a result of extensive research had resulted in the less tricky adoption of the arch as the fundamental differentiation than that of the arch taken in association with the hypertrophy of the paired triangular hyaline cartilage; this spared one being hypocritical, and the unfortunate Roman nose could be placed among the numerous mutations of the Greco-Nordic.

Upon reading this particular section in the proofs, and re-reading it, the professor became pensive. As a result of the revisions introduced, changing one or two things within the description of the Greco-Nordic nose itself obviously followed as well. Without diverging from its ideal ancient rectitude, it was necessary to make certain concessions in favor of the more prevalent, let's say even the more vulgar, of its features.

The prototype for this most widely disseminated Aryan nose could be served magnificently by the nose of Professor Kallenbruck himself, impeccably straight, though a touch meaty, with a slight thickening toward the end.

In order to adhere in this very case to the very rigors of science, the professor extruded from a drawer a pair of sliding compasses, used in such cases by anthropometrists, and he went over to the mirror in preparation to conduct the requisite measurements before it.

But, looking into the mirror, he took a step back and let the pair of compasses fall with a clatter.

Peering at him from the mirror was his own somewhat fat and flabby face, with thinning hair combed onto the temples and a short, neatly clipped mustache in the national fashion. Yet above the mustache, in place of the familiar straight nose lightly frosted with blackheads, a huge, hooked conk of unabashedly Semitic appearance loomed between frightened eyes.

The professor pulled at the nose with his hand, hoping that what he saw was the result of some form of optical illusion or a momentary hallucination. But alas!! His fingers were groping a gigantic fleshy schnoz!

This was not even a Roman arch — this was a whole hump, insolently protruding from between baggy eyes, a resilient lump of alien meat, a tight fitting ominous protuberance of paired triangular cartilage.

Professor Kallenbruck was a believer. Therefore, there was nothing in the least bit shameful or surprising that, in having misgivings as to the reliability of his own senses, he instinctively raised his eyes to heaven and spat into the corner three times in succession.

When the professor once again looked into the mirror, he witnessed that a third of his face was occupied, as before, by a bulbous Semitic nose, red with barely discernible purplish veins. Even the professor's face itself, always open and good-natured, one exuding pure-blooded German nobleness, had suddenly acquired an insidious Semitic expression.

He spat once again in anger and turned away in vexation from the mirror.

Not losing hope that everything was not what it appeared to be — possibly he was simply suffering from a higher than normal temperature — Professor Kallenbruck extracted a thermometer and placed it under his armpit. With eyes closed he counted to a thousand. The thermometer showed 97 degrees.

The professor again stepped up to the mirror and in despair tugged with two fingers at the inscrutable, uninvited nose. The nose didn't even quiver, obviously it had no intention of separating itself from its chosen resting place on the professor's face. What is more, having taken the caress of Kallenbruck's two fingers to be a naturally base gesture, it good-naturedly released two dewdrops which the professor, out of an innate sense of order, was forced there and then to wipe away with the fully understandable disgust each and every one of us would feel at having to wipe away someone else's snot.

It was now that even Kallenbruck's iron nerves gave way and he started to cry as a result of the horrific realization that he had blown the newly appeared Jewish nose as if it had been his very own, while the tears peacefully flowed through the tear duct beneath the lower nasal cavity as if they had known the route from birth and had in no way noticed any change whatsoever.

Somebody knocked at the door of the room.

Professor Kallenbruck, in horror, covered his nose with his

hand and looked unfavorably at the door. Seeing the man standing on the threshold he let out a cry of unexpected joy and flung himself on the new arrival with open arms.

And truly, providence could not have conceived of anything more apt: for at the moment of this trying ordeal it had granted him a friend.

•

Herr Theodor von der Pfordten, a member of the Judicial Board, stopped him with a motion of his hand and, placing his hands on Kallenbruck's shoulders, gently turned his face toward the light. Attentively, as would a doctor, he examined the professor's nose, turning his gray head this way and that, as if he wished to inspect the phenomenon from all possible angles. Finally, taking a few steps back and placing his hands behind his back, he reproachfully shook his head.

"Oh Theodor!" Kallenbruck exclaimed choking back the welled-up tears, "can't you see what has happened to me? And literally just a minute before you arrived. I myself couldn't believe my own eyes. Tell me — how could it have come about? Do you suppose the like has ever happened to anyone before?"

Herr von der Pfordten, without invitation, sank himself into an armchair and, crossing his legs, tapped a cigarette against the lid of his cigarette case.

"Yesss . . . ," he drawled with self-importance and thoughtfully pursed his lips.

Having said that, he again sank into a prolonged silence, occasionally puffing into the air perfect smoke rings — the celebrated Pfordten smoke rings that sticklers at the Gentlemen's Club would demand to be speared by the dozen on a billiard cue.

Professor Kallenbruck stood frozen stiff, not letting his gaze fall from the pursed lips of his friend in the hope that just then the sweet balsam of comfort would flow over his most troubled heart.

"There wasn't by any chance Jewish ancestry in your family on your father's side or, perhaps, on your mother's side?" uttered von der Pfordten, a member of the Judicial Board.

Professor Kallenbruck sat down on a chair in surprise.

"Theodor!" he exclaimed reproachfully, "How could you say such things! You personally knew my whole family. Was my late father not a close friend of your late father?"

"Maybe some grandfather or great-grandfather or other, whom I did not have the pleasure to know?" von der Pfordten added coldly.

"You're insulting me!" fumed the professor straightening his chest. The huge hooked nose on his pale Aryan face even reddened in indignation

"I didn't expect that from you, Theodor!"

"Oh, you know, in these times of ours . . . ," said his friend shrugging his shoulders.

"Quite, but this is contrary to common sense. Is it really possible that at the age of fifty one's nose can suddenly change?"

"Of course! It's quite possible." The gray gentlemen pressed with devastating certitude. "The majority of inherited characteristics become evident only in one's mature years. The whole matter lies in one's genetic predisposition."

"But with me, I swear to you — this all happened quite suddenly. I'd only just had lunch with the family, had sat down with a cup of coffee in order to peruse the proofs and suddenly . . ."

"It's always like that," confirmed the honorable member of the Judicial Board inexorably. "Constitutional features sometimes make themselves apparent even at a more advanced age than yours. For example, take my late grandfather, a renowned bon vivant and special advisor — Albert von der Pfordten, the permanent ambassador of His Excellency the King of Prussia to the Turkish court — in his sixtieth year a most nasty lump suddenly appeared on his forehead. And why not? Having rummaged in our family chronicles he established that just such a lump had featured above the left eye of his great-grandfather, a knight of the Maltese Order, Gustav von der Pfordten, who, in the words of the chronicles of the time, was even forced to have helmets made of a specific shape."

"All right, but a lump's one thing and a nose something else entirely . . . ," Kallenbruck said in weak defense, "there was never such a nose among any of my ancestors."

"It can all be verified," proposed the honorable member of the Judicial Board helpfully. "There is nothing simpler, for it is possible to establish one's exact genealogy by consulting the documents held in the civil records."

Herr von der Pfordten reached for his gold watch and rose from the armchair.

"It's still not too late. We can go there now and clear the matter up, without putting it off."

"Excellent, let's go!" Kallenbruck agreed hastily, though without any particular enthusiasm, "At the very least you will be shown the absurdity of your insinuations. But . . . how am I going to go out to the street with a nose like this?"

"Pull up your collar. Dusk is falling after all."

Professor Otto Kallenbruck, muffled up to his eyes in a scarf, with the collar of his overcoat turned up, allowed his friend to go first and followed him out onto the stairs.

He no longer thanked providence that at this dark hour von der Pfordten had been sent to him. He would have most willingly gotten rid of this persistent gentleman. Instead of comfort there arose in his soul a venomous mass of doubt. He thought with horror that the extraordinary misfortune that had befallen him, which could have been kept secret for a certain time, would now become the common knowledge of the whole town. Pfordten would trumpet it at every corner, which given his extensive connections in leading Party circles would not be particularly difficult for him to do.

If anyone else were to spread such an improbable rumor he might not be believed. But Theodor von der Pfordten, the author of the first National Socialist constitution, a leading light in the famous Beer Hall Putsch of November 9, 1923, in Munich, a participant in the unforgettable battle at the Feldherrnhalle — no, Theodor von der Pfordten would be believed by everyone without question. Here the professor suddenly had a strange and unheard-of thought.

"Wait, but von der Pfordten, if my memory serves me correctly, was killed during the battle at the Feldherrnhalle! . . ."

Professor Kallenbruck froze with one foot raised on a step of the staircase. He wanted to return and find in the cupboard *The National Socialists' Handbook* and look in the *Bibliographies of*

Our Leaders to see if his friend Theodor von der Pfordten had in fact died or survived.

But then the gray-haired gentleman descending the stairs before him turned around and stopped as well.

"Maybe you've reconsidered?" he asked with undisguised irony. "We can go back. I'm not insisting whatsoever."

"No, no, no, of course not," said Kallenbruck hurriedly.

He proceeded to shuffle down the steps, not taking his unfriendly stare off the armored back of von der Pfordten's head. In the opening between the brim of the reddish-brown castor oil colored bowler and the starched collar there bulged a neck — swollen, pink, and folded.

•

Outside it was drizzling. In the thin twilight the streetlights suddenly came on. The streetlamps stood in two rows like lanky soldiers in steel helmets, flashing out in the dark under the beam of a searchlight. Professor Kallenbruck had the impression he was being led through a military formation.

At the crossroads two corporation members in little colored caps were systematically and unenthusiastically beating a small man with canes. The man was shielding his head with his hand, and the youth in the green velvet cap was saying over and over as he beat him: "Cross over to the other side when you see us walking, you damned Yid! Stop getting in our way!"

A third young man in a little red cap was standing somewhat further off in the pose of an objective observer, limiting himself to laconic advice:

"Hit him on the bridge of the nose!" Or: "Smash him once again on the left ear!"

In the center of the intersection stood a policeman in a polished helmet, unruffled and motionless like a statue, his rubber truncheon hanging coquettishly from his belt.

Poor Professor Kallenbruck, his eyes buried in the scarf, sidled past the occupied members of the corporation. He hastened his step, hoping to catch up with von der Pfordten, who had gotten ahead of him. Yet he in turn had also hastened his step, and Kallenbruck understood that his friend deliberately had no intention of walking with him.

Having passed through one more quarter, Herr von der Pfordten turned into the gateway of a large, poorly lit garden. Judging by its location this was the Tiergarten, although it was more like a botanical garden. A fact borne out by the trees growing there, trees of the most fantastical and varied forms.

Found here were colossal trees, like the baobab, thin and tall trees, like the cypress, trees that were branchy below and barren at the top, which gave the appearance of growing upside down, and trees that were the opposite, plucked at the base and shaggy on the top like chamaerops, and those doubled up to one side like huge haloxylon saxaul bushes and spherical ones as if clipped by the skillful hand of a gardener. All the trees were hung from top to bottom either with cones or with fruit, the poor light not allowing one to make out exactly which.

A circular kiosk full of windows loomed in the middle of a graveled square.

Herr von der Pfordten stopped at one of the windows and awaited the panting Kallenbruck.

"Here you can obtain the sort of information you require." He showed the professor the illuminated window and the clearly visible head of a fiery red-headed, fat-faced clerk with ears like Kaiser Wilhelm. Freckles graced the clerk's face like copper pfennigs on a tray.

"What's this?" asked the surprised Kallenbruck, "You've brought me to peruse census documents?"

"Absolutely."

"But if I'm not mistaken this is the Tiergarten?" said the professor perplexed.

"You are by no means mistaken. The Tiergarten was indeed here before, but we've changed it into a genealogical garden."

"A ge-ne-a-lo-gi-cal garden?" asked Kallenbruck in disbelief

"Exactly so. Have you really not heard about it? This wondrous achievement of our city's commercial policies? It is a genuine triumph for our administration. Rather than having to rummage through mismanaged files of births and deaths scattered around dozens of archives, you simply come here! Every Berliner can find his genealogical tree. It visually depicts each and every lineage all the way back to ten generations. All you have to do is fill in this form."

Pfordten pushed one of the forms lying in front of the window toward Kallenbruck and, having dipped a fountain pen, obligingly gave it to the professor.

"If you would do the honor, here your first name, surname, year and place of birth, your parents' first names, your mother's maiden name . . . The rest you don't have to fill out. Below: the subject of the application, you should underline the first question: 'Has the person indicated any ancestors of Jewish origin?'

That's it. Ten pfennigs for the application . . . My dear fellow, if you'd be so kind!"

Professor Kallenbruck looked with trepidation at the opening jaws of the pneumatic tube into which the bored, red-mustached clerk mechanically dropped his application. The tube swallowed and closed.

The professor sank onto a bench in exhaustion.

In exactly five minutes the clerk called him by his surname and handed him the completed application form. On the reverse of the questionnaire there appeared:

"The grandfather of the named person on his father's side: Herman Kallenbruch, son of Isaac Kallenbruch and Devorah, née Hershfinkel. Born in 1805 in Solingen. In 1830 moved to Berlin. In 1845 converted to the evangelical religion and changed his surname from Kallenbruch to Kallenbruck. See genealogical tree 783211 (section XXV, alley 18).

"This isn't true! This is slanderous!" Kallenbruck started to yell, waving the piece of paper in front of the mustache of the indifferent clerk. The scarf wrapped around the professor's face uncoiled and indignantly palpitated in the wind. "How dare you! I knew my grandfather personally!"

The clerk raised up his bored eyes.

"I would ask you not to cause a disturbance," he said sternly, "if you don't believe our report, then buy yourself a mirror."

Professor Kallenbruck hurriedly hid his ill-fated Semitic nose in his scarf and, without a word, moved away from the window.

"Let's go and find your genealogical tree," said von der Pfordten, pulling him by the sleeve, "the location of the alley is shown exactly. There cannot be any mistakes in the genealogical tree. Each month they enter in the necessary corrections on the basis of newly discovered documents."

He hauled behind him the haggard and hunched Kallenbruck into a labyrinth of dimly lit alleys . . .

"Here," exclaimed the complaisant member of the Judicial Board. He stopped at a huge tree, similar to an ordinary fir tree, hung from top to bottom with cones.

"Now let's see. At the bottom on a plate with the number there should be a light socket."

Herr von der Pfordten leaned forward. He clicked the switch and the tree blazed with a bright electric light.

"Now just feast your eyes on that!"

Professor Kallenbruck screwed up his eyes at the unexpected brightness.

The sight was similar to a real Christmas tree. What the poor professor had taken in the gloom to be fir cones turned out now in the light to be little human figures made of plastic, clothed in painstaking detail according to the fashion of their era. On the twigs and branches to the left solemnly sat, like canaries, tiny burghers in yellow waistcoats and checked matrons in tall caps similar to the hoopoe's. On a stripped top branch, solitary as a brown owl, sat the incorrigible bachelor Uncle Gregor, thin with a huge head and sumptuous gray whiskers. Wizened Aunt Gertrude in her customary black skirt with a tail like a wagtail's cast indignant looks from her twig perch at her chilly, morose spouse, Uncle Paul, as if it was he and no one else who had placed her in such an uncomfortable position.

But to the right, oh my God! To the right suspended by the necks (obviously in belated punishment for the malicious harm to the German race) hung whole garlands of sad little Jews in skullcaps and gaberdines, one even — the professor was to remember this especially clearly — decked out in a genuine shtreimel.

Poor Professor Kallenbruck gave out a heart-rending cry and, covering his face with his hands, fainted.

·

On coming to he realized that he was sitting on a bench. In front of him stood Theodor von der Pfordten and, through his gesticulating, it was obvious that he had for a long time been trying to convince the professor about something that was highly pressing.

". . . And I was just getting at that, in the name of that drop of German blood which flows in your veins, you should make the decision without a moment's hesitation. Remember your own great words on the necessity to free the German nation of inferior elements! Was it not you who wrote about the heroes of the Great War as invalids, that people who in the name of the defense of the Fatherland had once shown courage and contempt for death should display the same again, taking their own lives in order to stop being a burden on the Third Reich?"

"No, it was not I who wrote that, I can assure you! That was Ernst Mann!" the professor attempted to object.

"All the better. I'm glad that these inspired words come from a pure-blooded German. Though in the discussion about inferior beings you were in complete agreement with Ernst Mann, with Professor Lenz and other genuine Germans. You even publicly defended their point of view. Was this not the case?"

"Yes, it was . . ." Kallenbruck confirmed despondently.

"You see! Just imagine how the enemies of National Socialist Germany would be gladdened and how they would be uplifted in knowing that one of the leading theorists and ideologists of racism has turned out to be . . . a Jew. You yourself understand that you must disappear, and disappear with as little fuss as possible before this whole matter becomes public knowledge. I could lend you my revolver, but too obvious a suicide would also be utilized by our enemies to launch fresh attacks on the Third Reich. The most sensible of all would be if you were to give your death the innocent coloring of an unfortunate accident. I recommend you throw yourself under a train or drown yourself in the Spree. Everyone knows your passion for fishing, and this would not arouse any particular suspicions."

"But my wife, my children!" groaned the professor in despair.

"Oh, we won't neglect them. You can rest assured of that. We will transfer your children after some time to special schools . . ."

"To special schools? But they sterilize them there!" implored Kallenbruck.

"You do understand that we cannot allow any further elements of Jewish origin to contaminate the German race. In your last book you quite correctly dealt with this question . . . As far as your wife is concerned she, as a blameless German and one who is still relatively young, will be able to give Germany more than one dashing Aryan heir. After your death we will find an appropriate husband for her. Herr Oswald von Wildau, the registrar, a magnificent example of a pure-blooded German, has always, it appears, been interested in her."

"Oswald von Wildau!" exclaimed the professor in outrage, "but he's married!"

"A trifle," replied von der Pfordten shrugging his shoulders, "and look who's talking? Professor Kallenbruck! Surely it was you who irrefutably proved in your last book that in the interests of racial purity the circle of producers should be limited to a small number of chosen males?"

"No, I beseech you, it was not I who wrote that! You've gotten it mixed up! That was Mittgard."

"Magnificent. But you did quote the man in your book. Did you not refer more than once to his 'The Route for the Regeneration of the German Race'?"

The professor humbly hung his head. He sat there squirming on the bench, as if disappearing into the collar of his coat. There was absolutely no point in contesting his own arguments. Moreover, after everything that had happened, there was no way for him to escape Theodor von der Pfordten . . .

Then, as the last ray of hope, the strange thought again flashed into Kallenbruck's head "And what if von der Pfordten had really died in the battle at the Feldherrnhalle? . . ." It even seemed to the professor that he could recall an obituary that had appeared in some vile opposition rag:

"A member of the Judicial Board, Herr Theodor von der Pfordten, the author of the illustrious National Socialist Constitution (which declared as outside the law a third of Germany's population, the killing of whom on sight was permitted to anyone!) has died. Oh the irony of fate! At the hand of the arm of the law, he was killed during the Beer Hall Putsch by a stray bullet, without being able to see his bloodthirsty constitution come into effect."

Professor Kallenbruck racked his memory. Did this just seem to be the case or had it actually happened? He was no longer listening to what von der Pfordten, who had not stopped appealing to his drop of German blood, was saying.

The professor had decided to bide his time and to flabbergast him with an unexpected question. If Pfordten was embarrassed, it would mean that he had in fact died, and then his evidence and his broad connections would not be so dangerous.

"I think I've told you everything that I'm obliged to say," said von der Pfordten pulling on gloves and bowing, "you will forgive me if I do not shake your hand in farewell. You surely understand that this would be contrary to my beliefs. Do pay heed to my friendly advice and do it this very evening, the sooner the better. I should warn you: should you not have the manliness to kill yourself the Party will be forced to assist you in the matter . . ."

"This is easy for you to say," Kallenbruck shot back in a last attempt at self-defense, not taking his eyes off Pfordten, "if I am not mistaken you were once personally assisted in this matter by a certain policeman. For you've been dead a long time already, Herr von der Pfordten!"

Kallenbruck moved forward in anticipation of the blow's impact.

"Genuine National Socialists do not die," replied von der Pfordten evasively, raising his bowler.

He turned and slowly disappeared into the gloomy depths of of an alley, leaving Kallenbruck still racked with doubt and in a tormented state of uncertainty.

Left alone, Professor Kallenbruck sat for a long time burdened by bitter reflection.

"When all's said and done the Party could make an exception for me given my service . . ." he said to himself after conflicting deliberation. "Maybe I should secure an audience with the Führer? Did the Zarathustra of National Socialism, Friedrich Nietzsche, not come from the Polish family of Nietski? Polish origins, if examined, are only a little better than Jewish ones. Add to Nietzsche's Polish origins his clearly expressed schizophrenia and the chances become almost equal . . . my God!" the professor roused himself, "I've even started to think like a Jew! Would I really have dared earlier to have thought about our great teacher in such a way. No, von der Pfordten is right! The inherited Jewish venom has already poisoned my German soul. I am no longer the master of my own thoughts. There is no salvation for me! If I don't do away with myself then they will surely do the job for me . . ."

With a heavy sigh he rose from the bench and, stooping, dragged himself off in the direction of the Spree. But his feet took him out of habit toward the Löwenbräu beer hall.

The clock face on the corner showed 7.

Yes, this was exactly the usual time when the regulars of the circular table at the Löwenbräu, founding members of the Society for the Struggle for German Racial Purity, would gather around a tankard or two to chat about important matters and to discuss the movement's current issues.

Just yesterday he had sat in his comfy armchair, having

Professor Sebastian Müller to his left, and to his right the gallant Fabricius Himmelstock, the editor of *The German Medical Weekly* and the author of the much discussed "Eugenic Analysis of the Composition of the Families of the Entire Prussian Police." He had sat and calmly discussed with them the urgent measures for the rectification of the catastrophic statistics, according to which the families of Prussian policemen multiply at a rate three times slower than that of ordinary workers.

On seeing the sign "Löwenbräu," Professor Kallenbruck was overwhelmed by a whirl of obtrusive recollections, which brought tears of tender emotion to his eyes. They overwhelmingly tugged him once more to cast a farewell glance, even if only through the window, at the interior of the familiar beer hall and his colleagues all assembled around the table.

Yes, they were sitting there as usual, around their favorite table with its customary "reserved" sign. The professor grew agitated seeing his empty chair. Knowing the inherent punctuality of Kallenbruck, his colleagues were surely at this very moment wondering what might have kept him from joining them.

The assembly was almost complete. Only the dashing Doctor Himmelstock was missing. He was obviously detained in his editorial office. The amber nectar shone golden in massive cut-glass tankards. The poor professor could distinctly sense in his mouth the bittersweet taste of the beer, and he moved his tongue over his lips.

Herr Noldtke, the justice, was holding in his hands a plump unopened book and, striking it with his palm, was showing something to the round-faced Professor Müller, with his pastoral halo of gray hair disheveled around his bald patch.

Professor Kallenbruck strained on tiptoes, clinging to the windowpane in his desire to catch the title of the work. The touch of the cold glass instantly transported him from the realm of sweet daydreams to that of gloomy reality.

"What are you doing here?" came a voice from behind his back. Professor Kallenbruck turned around.

In front of him stood the dashing Doctor Himmelstock, as always immaculately turned out in a new felt hat, slightly cocked backward.

"Are you blind?" He pointed with his cane at the sign on the window: NO JEWS ALLOWED. "I would have thought it was clear?"

". . . You . . . don't recognize me?" stuttered Kallenbruck perplexed.

"I do not and cannot possibly have any acquaintance among the representatives of your race!" Himmelstock looked him up and down. "Move off and don't spoil the view of the street for us!" He pushed Kallenbruck aside with his cane and disappeared behind the doors of the beer hall.

Professor Kallenbruck recoiled, brushing against one of the passersby, who pushed him away with such force that the poor academic was sent sprawling to the approving laughter of the assembled bystanders. From the force of hitting the pavement the professor's false teeth went flying, and he had to crawl on all fours after them, but someone had the foresight to kick them into the middle of the street under the wheels of the cars driving up and down.

Professor Kallenbruck thought he could drown himself perfectly well without teeth and, getting to his feet, he hurriedly turned into the first narrow side street. Trying hard to make his way unnoticed, he found himself after a few minutes by the Spree.

The oily patches of the streetlights floated on the black surface of the river.

The professor stopped on a bridge.

The water gurgled below, performing a distinct swallowing motion. The waves crowded around the piers of the bridge as if awaiting Professor Kallenbruck and, not put off by his presence, were already relishing the somewhat stout body, well preserved for its fifty years.

Such coarse indifference for human feelings was outrageous to the professor.

He quickly crossed the bridge, having decided to do away with himself in some other place. He went down onto the embankment and for a long time walked along the river, stopping from time to time in his search for an appropriate spot.

The river ran ahead and licked its lips in anticipation, awaiting him at every bend.

After a lengthy search, he finally selected a secluded nook for himself – a genuine haven for a suicide – when he heard the tread of striding feet and the sound of choral song.

This was his favorite song – the "Horst Wessel Song," time and again performed at the Löwenbräu beer hall with unfailing success and not without the participation of Professor Kallenbruck himself. He mentally sang the first lines.

Suddenly he noticed that the previously deserted embankment was quickly coming to life. People were running along the pavement and road in all directions. The windows and gates of the houses banged shut.

Unexpectedly Professor Kallenbruck found himself amid the running people. Somebody shouted in his ear in Yiddish. "Why are you just standing around?!? Run!"

The professor wanted to protest his being taken for a Jew, but had no time to. Seized by fear and panic, without thinking, he set off at a gallop after the others.

The number of those running melted away, dissolving into side streets and gateways. Professor Kallenbruck had no idea where to turn, he didn't even know exactly where he was. Exhausted, short of breath, he lent against a streetlight greedily gasping for air.

"Run!" shouted a man who darted past.

The professor obediently ran a few more steps and finally, devoid of strength, sank down to the edge of the pavement.

The man who had outstripped him stopped in hesitation, turned back, and put Kallenbruck on his shoulders before running on.

They turned into some narrow side streets, and the man with Kallenbruck on his back dove into a big set of gates that reeked of garlic and cats. He set Kallenbruck down on a black staircase in the second courtyard. Both panted long and rapidly, listening out for the crescendoing chanting of the "Horst Wessel," a lover of poetry, wine, and the ladies.

The song rumbled past under the rattle of whistles and the sound of broken glass, and then it gradually began to recede into the distance.

"Let's go," whispered the man.

He got up, motioning to Kallenbruck to follow. They clambered up the narrow steep staircase to the third floor. The professor was having difficulty. He hadn't run so much since his student days.

Entering a dark corridor, the man knocked on one of the doors. It did not open at once. Those behind the door questioned the newcomer for a long time in Yiddish. Finally the bolt was drawn back.

•

A long table stood in the room Kallenbruck entered with the stranger. On the table two candles were burning in two seven-branched candelabras. There was a telephone, two plates of matzo, an open Talmud of colossal dimensions, and a large pile of gold coins. Twelve decrepit Jews wearing shtreimels were seated at the table. The Jews had gray beards down to their waists and long earlocks stretched out like springs.

On seeing Professor Kallenbruck, all twelve of the old men jumped playfully from their seats, most unexpectedly for their age, and started to sing in unison:

> We are a dozen, a dozen are we
> Wise men of Zion!
> We need the whole world, yes, indeed!
> On it we will dine . . .

Having finished singing they performed several gluttonous movements with their jaws and chattered their teeth as if this eating up of the world were to occur in a single sitting. The old men danced a jig in time and then as if on command again sat at the table in unison and sank into a deathly silence.

"Who are you?" asked the most decrepit Jew. Hairs were sprouting out of his ears and nose, gray hairs like wormwood, and the bushy white eyebrows dropping onto his eyes appeared to be a second mustache growing by mistake above his eyes.

"Who am I?" dolefully mumbled Kallenbruck, "yesterday I was still a rich and respected man, the head of a family and the pride of my friends. And now? Now I'm simply a poor Jew."

"What misfortune befell you?" solemnly asked the old man with the two mustaches in response, as if following a ritual routine.

"Oh, Wise Man of Zion, sir!" Kallenbruck sighed heavily, "I have had such misfortune befall me that if I were to tell you, you wouldn't believe me. I had a beautiful Aryan nose — what a nose — and they've gone and changed it for this pumpkin. I had a wife who is still young and quite a looker, and they've taken her away and have ordered her to have children with a married registrar, Herr Oswald von Wildau. I had children — and what children they were! And they're going to take them to a special school and have them sterilized so that they can't reproduce. I had fame and was honored, but now I can't even show myself on the street lest some old pen pusher or other knock my teeth out or soil my clothes. Tell me, oh Wise Men of Zion, was there ever a man on this earth of ours more unlucky than I?"

At this, all twelve Jews nodded their heads compassionately, and the elder with the face grown over with wormwood asked for a third time.

"Would you like to take revenge on those who have humiliated you?"

"Would I like to take revenge? And wouldn't you take revenge for your ruined life, for your desecrated wife, for your sterilized children? But tell me, oh Wise Man of Zion, what can I do?"

"All right," nodded the old man, "we will help you. Only swear that you will always remain with us and that you will never tell anyone anything under any circumstances whatsoever. There on the plate is matzo. It has been kneaded with the blood of eminent Nazis, shot by Herr Hitler himself. Break off a piece and eat!"

"The devil take them all!" exclaimed the professor, and he broke off a large piece of matzo and swallowed it without chewing.

He felt that his thoughts were suddenly filled with a hitherto unknown cunningness and guile, and that a still vague but uncommonly devilish plan had started to take root in his head.

"And how will you take revenge on them?" asked the old man.

"Wait, just wait, I've got an idea!" exclaimed Kallenbruck, inspired. "They have established a genealogical garden where on the basis of the census they create an exact genealogical register of every German all the way to ten generations back. Each month, as new documents are discovered, they amend and update the genealogical trees. Why don't we bribe all the archivists in Germany to enter into the registers of births one Jewish ancestor for each pureblooded German! Tomorrow the whole of Germany will know that Göring is in fact not Göring but Hering – a simple Jewish herring – and that there is not a single National Socialist whose grandfather, or at a pinch great-grandfather, was not a Jew!"

On hearing Kallenbruck's words all twelve of the wise men started to dance a Bolshevik Hopak.

When the first outburst of general joy had died down, the old man with the double mustache turned to Kallenbruck:

"Until now we were twelve sages of Zion. Each of us has thought up no end of schemes for the ruin of the Christian world, but no one has come up with a plan of such genius. You deserve the esteemed status of Sage of Zion. From this day forward we will be thirteen!"

All the old men fell into such rejoicing it was a long time before they managed to calm down. They placed a satin caftan around the professor's shoulders and a large shtreimel on his head and seated him in the most honored place.

The professor was suprised to notice a long silvery beard sprouting from his shaven chin like the water from the biblical rocks after Moses's staff had struck them.

When silence had settled, the old men began to discuss the details of the plan for revenge.

"If one day one Jewish forebear were to appear for each and every German, then all of them, like it or not, would have to come to terms with it, and then there would be no discord whatsoever," said the dark radiant old man with the long fangs of gray whiskers that resembled those of a walrus. "Therefore, in my understanding of the matter, it would not be necessary to make this entry for everyone, but gradually, starting with only National Socialists, and then not all of them at once but initially only those who are the most deserving."

Everyone agreed with this judicious remark, and it was decided to enter, as a start, Jewish ancestry only for those members of the Nazi Party with membership cards numbered from 1 to 10,000.

It was decided to set about bribing archivists as soon as possible. The old men swiftly shoveled up the gold coins from the table and, having counted them into their pockets, they started to sing in unison:

Hi, Zion, shine with delight!
Our body has been increased
To the tune of one wise man
Lamtsa dritsa, ram pan pan!

Then, having performed a few tricks and pulled their hats down over their eyes, they all disappeared together through the doorway, leaving Kallenbruck alone at the empty table with the telephone and the seven-branched candelabra.

The professor would have called after the whisker-eyebrowed old man to ask if he was to stay there or to go with them, but the room was already empty.

The candles burnt dimly, winking at the professor and dripping stearin tears onto the deserted table, onto the plate with the matzos, onto the solitary forgotten little circle of gold.

The professor started to feel not quite himself. An idea flashed through his head — had they entrapped him? This thought clotted into a panic-ridden conviction when, in the corridor, the bell started to ring persistently without letting up.

The professor flung himself about, hitting the candelabra with his elbow and knocking the candles over.

The candles flickered and went out. He was left in complete darkness.

Now it seemed to him the ringing was not coming from the

corridor but from the telephone on the table. With shaking hands he fumbled in the dark, groping on the table but failing to locate the telephone and hurting his finger on something. Eventually his hand grasped the receiver. He yanked it to himself and raised it to his ear . . .

"Hello? Who's speaking?"

•

"Herr Professor Kallenbruck?" came a familiar voice from the receiver. "Good evening! This is Doctor Himmelstock speaking. What's up with you today? Why are you not at the Löwenbräu? We've been sitting here without you for an hour and a half now. Finally we decided to give you a call. Are you all right?"

"Me? That is, how's that? . . ." mumbled Kallenbruck.

"A pity you decided not to drop in for a pint. Herr Justice Noldtke was in excellent form and spoke about the most interesting of things . . . apropos, I really ought to congratulate you, the Führer was most taken by your book about the endogenous minus-variants of Jewry. He read it yesterday in bed until two in the morning . . . Well, when will we see you? Tomorrow? Come on, it's a must. There are so many new things to tell! . . . If I hurry I'll catch the end of your lecture today . . ."

The caller hung up.

Professor Kallenbruck continued to sit for a few minutes in the dark with the receiver to his ear. Then he groped to return it to its stand, and his hand fumbled for the light switch.

A table lamp flashed on. Screwing up his eyes from the light, the professor surveyed his old, quite familiar study – his desk, the telephone, an ashtray, a cigar box, the proofs spread out on the desk:

"As opposed to the Roman nose and other numerous variations on the classic Greco-Nordic nose type, the Semitic nose is characterized first and foremost by its visible hypertrophy at the paired triangular hyaline cartilage formed in conjunction with the protruding arch . . ."

Professor Kallenbruck with a single leap jumped out from behind the table and rushed over to the mirror. A vocal sigh of relief shook his heavy build.

Between his baggy eyes, above his mustache, neatly clipped in the national fashion, rose the impeccably straight nose, slightly widening at the end, of the Kallenbruck family. The starkness and purity of his Aryan lineage could not arouse any doubts whatsoever.

The professor drew his palm over his forehead:

"Phew! What vile rubbish a man can imagine!" He turned around to the table, glanced at an edition of *Völkischer Beobachter* with an announcement marked in red:

> *Tonight at 8 o'clock p.m., at the Club for Friends of Militant Eugenics, Professor Otto Kallenbruck Ph.D. will deliver a lecture on "The Semitic Nose as One of the Hereditary Minus-Variants of Jewry." Discussion to follow.*

The professor looked at his watch: "Oh no! It's ten to eight."

"Berta!" he called, opening the door to the corridor – "Berta! Give me my black frock coat and tell Mitzi to warm a glass of beer on the double."

"Light the top light, Berta!" ordered the professor, taking the frock coat from his wife's hand.

Having done up his tie, he glanced askance in the mirror at the light step of his wife, at the sluggish movement of her full hands brushing out the stubs from the ashtray.

"Berta!" he called to her, sticking in his tie pin, "just imagine for a moment the following most improbable situation — what would you do if your husband . . . — this is of course funny and absurd, but let's just suppose for a minute — what would you do if your husband turned out to be a Jew?"

"You do have an odd sense of humor, Otto!"

"But let's just imagine for a minute," persisted her spouse, "what would you do then?"

"Well, I'd get rid of him straight away of course."

"And would you not regret that you had children together, or feel nostalgic for all those long years you spent together?"

"My, how strange you are! For what reason should one feel sorry for a Jew?"

"And where would you go after leaving? To the registrar, Herr Oswald von Wildau?" asked Kallenbruck maliciously, unable to hide the bitterness in his voice.

"See how vicious you are!" said his wife, going red. "You ask me absurd questions only to wound me! Are you really going to be jealous of Herr von Wildau all your life?"

"Ha, ha! I'm only joking!" the professor began to laugh, "there's nothing to take offense over." He patted her on the cheek in a forced manner. "You answered as would befit a true German woman. Now go and fetch me my beer."

For no explicable reason, he felt growing irritation toward

this rotund, buxom woman, the mother of his three children, and preferred to be alone.

"Dad, here you go — your beer!" announced the youngest Kallenbruck, seven-year-old Willi, in a high little voice from the doorway as he passed the professor a steaming china mug on a tray.

The professor stroked the boy's fair hair and drained the mug in a single gulp.

"Dad, can I have that empty cigar box?" Willi asked, fingering the large bow on his chest.

The professor nodded affectionately — "Willi!" he stopped the little boy as he ran out with the cigar box toward the doorway, "come here. Tell me, let's imagine a most improbable situation — what would you do if suddenly your father turned out to be a Jew?"

The boy looked at his father inquiringly, hiding the box behind his back.

"I would call Fred and Trudi and we would lure him outside and we would bash in his head with a poker and then chuck him onto the rubbish heap," he said without pausing for thought while looking at his father with big enthusiastic eyes.

He continued to stand there clearly awaiting the well-earned reward — his father usually gave him twenty pfennigs for each and every correct answer. But this time Father was obviously distracted. Instead of giving his son twenty pfennigs, he simply said, not even looking in his direction: "Yes, yes, that's my boy! . . ."

And he ordered him to run to tell Mitzi to order the car.

A number of distinguished persons were already gathered in the Club for Friends of Militant Eugenics. Forcing his way through to his chair, Professor Kallenbruck shook the hands of dozens of well-wishers. Everyone knew what a glowing review the Führer himself had given his book, and so there was no end to the congratulations.

Professor Kallenbruck started his lecture with a tried and tested historical joke, one that had proved its worth in dozens of auditoriums. He announced that if the learned seventeenth-century Portuguese Jew, Isaac de la Peyrère (he placed the stress on "Isaac") had asserted that God had created Aryans and Semites not on the selfsame day then he, Kallenbruck, did not find any objections to the idea. He was even prepared to agree with I-ssa-c de la Peyrère that Aryans were created a day earlier than Semites. Undoubtedly God felt tired after five days of uninterrupted creativity, and the race produced by him on the sixth day was constructed out of not particularly quality material, which explains the low racial features today's Jews have inherited from their ancestors.

With his characteristic expressiveness he outlined for the auditorium the fundamental psychological traits of Jewry that were a result of pathological mutation not weeded out by natural selection.

He demonstrated the irrefutable fact established by Lenz and Luxemburger of the greater incident of psychiatric illnesses among Jews in comparison to representatives of the Nordic race. He referred to Gutmann, who considered flat-footedness to be an inherited feature peculiar to Jews. When at the very end he moved to the fundamental subject of the lecture, to the Semitic nose and its influence on the psychology of Jewry, the hall, as if bewitched, did not for a moment take its eyes off the lips of the eloquent professor.

Then something unexpected happened, about which the participants of this unusual lecture would discuss for a long time afterward in bewilderment and disbelief.

Coming to the descriptions of the Semitic nose with its characteristic arch, in conjunction with the hypertrophy of the paved triangular hyaline cartilage, the professor suddenly felt his own nose, stopped short, went pale, and, grabbing his nose, rushed there and then out of the hall with a terrible cry of "oy vey!"

At first, all those present took this to be a humorous intermezzo. Then the rumor spread that the professor, without coat or hat, had rushed out into the street and had darted off in an unknown direction.

A fifteen-minute break was called. When, however, after half an hour the professor had not returned, rumors ran rife among the public, and so to avoid undesired complications the evening was pronounced over. The promised discussion did not take place.

•

Here the strange story of Professor Kallenbruck comes to an end. However hard we have tried, we have been unable to discover anything more certain about his fate. Scant news has come out of Nazi Germany during this period. And as for unfortunate incidents that have occurred to members of the ruling party, knowledge about them has been kept, as one would expect, in the utmost secrecy.

From the scant and contradictory echoes that could have some relevance to Professor Kallenbruck, a note that appeared in Berlin newspapers on exactly the second day after the lecture at the Club for Friends of Militant Eugenics deserves our attention: according to the note the Tiergarten guards had apprehended the previous night an unknown elderly gentlemen climbing up a tree with an ax and chopping off the branches from one side of it. The person detained displayed signs of slight madness.

After the events described, a short announcement – devoid of commentary – quickly appeared in German opposition newspapers published abroad that the famous racist professor, Otto Kallenbruck, a member of the National Socialist Party, had, following his return from an academic research trip to twenty-three of Fascist Germany's concentration camps, gone out of his mind.

Incidentally, during these years German state officials and academics, champions of the law on obligatory sterilization, of the likes of Wilhelm Frick (before him – the Social Democratic member of the Reichstag A. Grotjahn), considered the overall number of defective individuals in one respect or another in Germany to be equal to a third of its entire population, which would have constituted more than twenty million people.[3]

More conservative in his estimates was Professor Fritz Lenz,

[3] A. Grotjahn. "Soziale Pathologie." Berlin, 1923.

who calculated the number to be twelve million at most.[4] This figure referred, it is true, to those years that preceded the establishment of the Nazi regime, during whose existence, judging by newspapers and official data, the number of mentally ill significantly increased.

According to the words of Doctor Falthauser, "in order to satisfy the need for psychiatric hospitals this would require construction of such a magnitude as to lead possibly to widespread social unrest."[5]

The splendid work of the German statistician G. Stecker, "The Statistical Comparison of Various Professions in Relation to their Affliction with Mental Illnesses," acted as a most calming influence on the agitated social opinion of European countries, which found these figures alarming.[6]

In accordance with these statistics, the percentage of primary mental illnesses for "businessmen living in retirement" constituted a mere 1.6%, for the more troubled profession of rentier 6.7%, and the percentage of simply unqualified workers reached a level of 39.5%.

Hence, according to the authoritative assertions of Stecker and other German statisticians, the overwhelming part of the mentioned twenty million was composed of psychologically defective proletarian elements, whose low racial characteristics made them especially susceptible to mental illness. Professor

---

[4] Fritz Lenz, Ph.D. "Menschliche Auslese und Rassenhygiene (Eugenik)." Lehmanns Verlag. München, 1931.
[5] "Zeitschrift fur psychiatr. Hygiene," V., Heft 2-4.
[6] Stecker. "Statistische Darstellung der Belastung mit psychischen Erkrankungen verschiedener Fachgruppen." "Psychiatr.-neurologische Wochenschrift" Nr. 18, 1933.

Otto Kallenbruck, Ph.D., on the basis of this data, represented a rare exception.

In a highly confidential statistical report prepared by the German secret police, among the fifty-six thousand incurable asocial elements, schizophrenics, epileptics and the like sterilized in 1934 in concentration camps, psychiatric hospitals, and special needs schools in Germany, the surname of a certain Kallenbruck was to be found. As a consequence of the absence of initials, however, it is difficult to establish whether this actually refers to Professor Otto Kallenbruck, Ph.D.

If this indeed happened to be the case, we would, despite the generally known attachment of authors to their heroes, abstain from cries of protest and indignation, remembering the words of the German Minister of Health, Doctor Reiter, whom Kallenbruck loved to quote:

"It is necessary to choose the healthy and to care about their propagation. For the sick can be left to their own devices – they merely burden society."[7]

For the sake of completeness, we shall add just one, unfortunately unverified, rumor that circulated in its time within the medical circles of Berlin: Professor Otto Kallenbruck, Ph.D., died of progressive paralysis.

If we follow the view of such an academic authority as Westhof, whose original opinion is of late increasingly less and less cited by German eugenicists, then it is impossible to deny this version's high plausibility. As is known, Westhof held the view that the higher a living creature has furthered itself along

[7] From a speech at the Congress of National Socialist Doctors [Kongress der nationalsozialistischen Ärzte] in Nuremberg (1933).

the ladder of development, then the more it will succumb to illness. In admitting progressive paralysis in particular as one of the indices of spiritual culture, Westhof considered it an especial privilege and proof of the spirituality of the German race. In his opinion: "All nations start to suffer from progressive paralysis in relation to their dealings with Germans. Even among Jews the frequency of progressive paralysis is conditioned by the same . . ."

AN ACCOUNT

Finally, one more piece of news has recently come to our attention that has compelled us again to think about Professor Kallenbruck and his extraordinary adventures.

On the basis of highly confidential reports, a great impression has been made within the ruling circles of the National Socialist Party by the sensational disclosures of a certain little known lawyer, a member of the Party, who in a secret memorandum addressed to the Führer himself has proven with documentation the Jewish origins of a large number of eminent Nazis.

Rumor has it that the special commission established to investigate the veracity of such a grave charge has not only confirmed these disclosures but with every month adds to them an ever-growing list of prominent National Socialists, the Jewish provenance of whom has virtually been proved on the basis of new documents found by archivists. To avoid a panic, information about the work of the commission is kept in absolute secrecy.

1936

THE CHIEF CULPRIT

The bare plain in front of the trench, swept clean by searchlights, dazzled with a dead, uniform radiance.

It was as if the enemy, having fallen back, had lost a needle here and decided to find it on this gloomy night. In the distance the howitzers sighed in wonder. The trench was quiet. The soldiers' teeth could be heard chattering softly from tension and fear.

"Over the top!"

No one stirred. Even the distant artillery fell silent, listening. An anxious stillness descended.

"God! Maybe they won't come! Maybe this time they won't come!"

But on the right flank, edging forward and getting tangled in the skirts of their greatcoats, they had already climbed onto the ridge of the embankment. The first man bent toward the ground and jumped down onto a patch of grass ablaze with light. And suddenly, as if to mark the difficulty of this acrobatic act, a drum roll of machine guns burst out in the hollow silence.

Men now ran like an uncoiled chain. All at once they started to fall, face downward, arms splayed, as if they had tripped on an invisible wire . . . Cramp gripping his whole body, he recoiled like a spring. He clambered up the embankment. The piercing beam of the searchlights slashed across his eyes. The earth shone like phosphorous.

He picked himself up and ran, almost on all fours, dragging his rifle butt along the ground. The air screeched mournfully, pricked by bullets. "If only there were a small shell crater!" There was no crater. It might have kept this terrible, harsh light from exposing him.

To the left, several steps away, a thin brown stump protruded from behind a knoll. A narrow strip of shadow streamed along the ground from the stump . . .

He crawled up to it and buried his face in it, pressing his whole body to the hillock. The desire to squeeze himself into the earth was so violent that for a moment it seemed the ground would yield and he would escape into it like a mole.

Boots and rifle butts ran past, jostling him. Someone tripped and crashed down on him with all his force. He raised his head a little. A young lieutenant looked at him, his eyes flashing, burning with light.

"Coward!" hissed the lieutenant, unfastening his holster . . .

. . . He awoke in a sweat, his face caked with dust from the straw. Squeezed into the corner, his nails shredded the pillows. For a long time he sat, breathing heavily, in no state to imagine where he was. Again that relentless dream!

It had started long ago, shortly after the end of that first, great war, which for him had ended somewhat earlier than for the rest. As luck would have it, he had been poisoned with gas, and had spent the following months almost comfortably, in an infirmary well away from the front lines. They had no idea the gas hadn't killed him, and then while he was in the hospital, as they were treating his punctured lungs, the war suddenly ended. Or so the papers claimed. In actual fact, it continued at night.

He had been out of action for several months, so each night it revenged itself on him. It forced him to relive again the hours of deadly fear, ordered him to die a hundred different ways, after he had cleverly wriggled his way out of a genuine death.

This continued for two whole years until, finally bored of these unreal dreams, war started up again for real. In truth of fact, he never really believed it had actually ended. Now he understood this had simply been a respite; he had received a two-year vacation to recover. (The boys from the front had been given only two weeks — he'd been lucky in this — but on the other hand, after returning to duty they had usually been killed without much ado, many on the very first day.)

The newspapers vied with each other in their efforts to convince the world that this was by no means the selfsame war, that it was a completely different war: a holy crusade in the defense of civilization against the barbarism advancing from the East. Resuscitated a mere two years earlier, independent Poland had a mission bestowed on it by fate to advance the outposts of the cultured West up to the Dnieper River. The press had written about the previous war in much the same way.

He knew, like a catechism, like the soldier's ten commandments the NCOs drummed into recruits, that every war is holy, that everyone fights in the defense of civilization, and that it's always necessary for someone somewhere to advance some outpost or other. He knew that newspapers were also NCOs, only for civilians, and he left the greenhorns to demonstrate their fighting spirit on the street with their marching songs. Once they sniffed the front, they'd soon be singing a different tune . . .

As far as he was concerned, he'd had his fill, until he'd vomited blood, and he was onto their cheap tricks.

In the bank where he worked as a junior bookkeeper, they looked at these matters differently. The majority of the petty clerks had long ago signed up as volunteers. The situation was becoming more and more delicate with each passing day. When the outposts of the cultured West were driven back from the Dnieper by the barbarians who were now rapidly approaching the gates of Warsaw, the senior accountant from another department gave him a resonant slap in front of all and called him a coward and a traitor.

He had to leave his job. He locked himself in and tried to sit out the affair at home. He had some savings, enough to see him through. He entertained the rather naïve belief then that they might just leave him in peace.

They discovered him at home and presented his draft notice. On the streets, disheveled, venerable ladies organized roundups of young men in civilian clothes and escorted them to the nearest police station, tearing off their ties as they went. There was simply nowhere to hide. One had only to set foot out on a street and it would snap shut like a mousetrap.

In the barracks they were issued French greatcoats and paraded for roll call. Those who had taken part in the previous war were lined up separately, equipped, and promised transfer the very next day to the trenches.

These people were remote and unfamiliar – apart from Jan Głowak. They had served for a time together in the same platoon and had lost each other in the Mazurian marshes.

They spent the night on plank bunks, trading wartime memories.

"I knew they wouldn't let up until they've killed us all!" Głowak said suddenly in the dead of night and, falling silent, added: "I've had enough!"

In the morning Głowak was nowhere to be found on the bunks. They discovered him in the latrine when the company assembled for dispatch. He was hanging by his trouser belt, attached to the flush mechanism – gangly and awkward in his long johns, with the purple shrapnel scar across his cheek. The purling water lapped at the big toes of his bony feet.

Thus he was to be remembered: outstretched and elongated, as if standing on tiptoe in the water.

The officer angrily cursed the deceased as a damned coward and ordered him to be taken to the morgue. It was no more than half an hour's truck ride to the forward positions, and this idiot Głowak could have waited!

Again war. The peaceful counter in the bank with its piles of ruled paper seemed from this vantage point a radiant mirage. And in fact, it was a mirage. Reality was here, endlessly shifting from animal fear, like a cork rammed down his throat, to absolute torpor: "The sooner the better! Let it be!" At night Jan Głowak, long and barefoot, with the purple scar across his cheek, walked on tiptoe like Christ over the bubbling water. It was fear that kept one from following in his footsteps . . .

. . . he came round in the lazaretto with a lump of white gauze in place of a head. From beneath the gauze a single eye, like a piece of coal set in a snowman, squinted amusingly. Again they spoke of how the war was over. He closed the eye and smiled to the gauze: same old story!

Within a few months he was released. The young hospital surgeon, a keen follower of new trends in medicine, had patched up his nose with a piece of thigh. The nose had mended almost perfectly, with only a slight tilt to the right. Given the conservative medical procedures then practiced, it was somewhat more difficult to repair the eye that had come out. A glass one would have to do. Blue and languid, the assistant surgeon assured him it was even more expressive and wistful than the right.

At home, having examined his slightly crushed face with its alarmingly fixed, staring eye, he grew somewhat melancholic. The promise of success in life, the alluring exterior which he had earlier so prized — they had even succeeded in taking this from him, eliminating it by the surgeon's knife.

In exchange, a faint hope remained: maybe now that he had just one eye, they would stop harrying him off to war. Yet aiming a rifle required shutting the left eye, making it superfluous to a soldier's needs. There was no point in holding out any hope.

The bank accepted him back as someone who had sacrificed for the motherland, his initial reluctance having been magnanimously forgotten.

The war wound down, as it were. It continued in snatches at night. During the day everyone, as if part of a prearranged plan, gave the impression that they knew nothing about it. People strolled down the streets, all dolled up, deliberately businesslike, or feigning indifference. Only certain individuals in the midst of this colorful crush, people in appearance no different than the rest, would suddenly give a knowing wink at one another with the convulsive grimace of shell shock, therein emphasizing how illusory this all was.

From time to time reminders of the "historical mission" and "outposts" would again creep into the papers. Smiling arrogantly, braided officers would saunter through the streets, striking the pavements with the dazzling scabbards of their long sabers that trailed behind them like trains. This meant that leave would soon be cancelled. Yet days and months passed, while the familiar white smears of the draft notices on the peeling walls of the houses ordered one to wait.

The war shifted to a new theater. Now it was raging in Morocco. The newspapers outdid one another in conveying the graphic details. Life in Warsaw resumed its normal course. Doughnuts were fried on Fridays at the home of the senior accountant. Miss Jadwiga, his daughter, would serve them at table. There was so much love and peace expressed in the eyes of Miss Jadwiga that by looking into them one could easily believe in eternal leave. He believed once again. They were married at the Church of the Blessed Virgin Mary.

The following day he was awoken by a stray bullet, which shattered the kitchen window and landed in a jar of jam. He leapt up in a confusion of emotions. The city shook to the sound of firing.

The newspapers then asserted that this was less a war than a moral revolution. The Marshall himself had decided to cure Poland, which his predecessors had allowed to become ill. The dead were relatively few, and all of them, regardless of rank and allegiance, were buried with the same military honors.

Alas, nothing was able to restore his shattered illusions! Family tranquility had been destroyed. Even the comforting information on identical honors being bestowed was unable to excite him . . .

Two years later — the war was now raging in China — he returned home unexpectedly to find a long saber in the hallway. A thickset officer, buttoning up his white summer uniform and adjusting his multi-strapped harness, gruffly expressed his readiness to give him whatever satisfaction he required, whereupon he gave his holster a lively pat and, picking up his saber, left the room in no particular hurry.

Everything would work itself out. Having failed to demand satisfaction from the burly officer he fell even lower in the eyes of his unfaithful wife, irreconcilable in matters of male honor. He well remembered the recent incident of an officer who had slain a civilian on the street with his sword, and the victim had not struck him or in any way shown him disrespect. The officer was vindicated by the court as having stood up for the honor of his uniform. His portrait was displayed in the window of a large photographic studio, complete with a bunch of roses.

Just then the newspapers brought news of a terrible explosion at a chemical plant in Hamburg. A huge cloud of phosgene had almost enveloped the town. Luckily the wind had been blowing in the opposite direction and had carried it out to sea. A group of day-trippers, forty miles from the city, hit the remains of the gas cloud two days later and dropped dead to a person, poisoned by the fumes. There could be no doubt: everything was starting afresh.

Though imminent, war was not to break out that year, nor the next. Anyone could see, however, that real preparations were being made. The newspapers were filled with reports on the European powers arming, and that not to respond would prevent Poland from fulfilling its historical mission.

Sometimes at night he thought that if the situation dragged on for three or four years his age would protect him from the draft. This illusory comfort was finally shattered when one day he read in an article by a highly authoritative military official that future wars would be directed not so much against enemy armies as against the enemy's civilian population – the chief culprit in maintaining the enemy's morale and economic power.

He was somewhat alarmed by the article: it appeared that without suspecting it he was the chief culprit, cause and abettor of destruction that had general staffs racking their brains!

Every day the newspapers brought stunning revelations about new super-powerful dreadnoughts, tanks, and bombers. From the cinema screen multistory battleships slowly swung the barrels of their guns toward him. All the machine guns and artillery pieces of the world pointed at him, only awaiting the pre-arranged signal. It was pointless to dream of salvation. Bayonet attacks began to resurface in his dreams.

The crumpled pillow – the sole witness to his fruitless attempts to squeeze himself into the ground – would look at him in the mornings with an ironic reproach: Had not yesterday's *Warsaw Courier* announced that the latest bombs, weighing a ton apiece, could crater the earth to a depth of eighty feet on impact? Gigantic bombers, heavyweight champions, could already carry a payload of up to twenty-five tons. A few planes of such caliber could destroy the entire city.

He would read every newspaper until it disintegrated in the sad hope that he would find at least a scrap of information about possible defense measures. The news was generally of little comfort. The English regretfully admitted that during the latest nighttime air drills, out of the one hundred planes that had simulated a raid on London, thirty-six reached their target undetected. If they had dropped real bombs, London would have been leveled.

One day, in a dry communiqué about a conference taking place in Geneva, where they were discussing the results of the latest air drills, he read in black-and-white that the conference had admitted that all existing means of anti-air defense were unreliable. The only effective defense measure recommended was a policy of reprisal – capital for capital: If you destroy Paris, I'll do Berlin! Such a measure would exterminate the chief culprit – the civilian – once and for all.

The military gentlemen, not confining themselves to the present, turned their eye to the future. They had all unanimously found current cities to be the failed crop of the dim-witted public. One military expert wrote that cities henceforth needed to be built deep underground in the form of complexes of concrete bunkers. Electricity and oxygen could be generated so the inhabitants would not face too great a hardship. As the construction of such cities would require a great deal of time, it would obviously have little effect on the approaching war, which would run its course regardless; but such an undertaking would be absolutely essential in the future. These gentlemen were quite confident that they would survive to see the war-after-next unscathed.

Some foreign colonel with an unpronounceable surname proposed the construction of human settlements in the form of scattered high-rise minarets placed at an appropriate distance from one another. He claimed they would present the least accessible target for aerial bombardment.

General Puderin, whose surname was easy to remember as it reminded one of "pudding," recommended, instead of cities as presently constituted, that hundreds of thousands of small fireproof houses made of steel and metalized wood be scattered on hillsides. Houses of this kind could be easily camouflaged, while the circulation of the mountain air would go a long way to protecting them against poisonous gases. Unfortunately, the attractive project of this nature-loving general was hardly feasible for countries lacking in high mountain areas, such as Poland. All of its population would be required to resettle to the Tatras, thus unavoidably creating an area of high population density — something far from desirable in matters of defense.

Though carried away with dreams of the war-after-next, the generals had in no way forgotten about the one that was approaching.

Gas shelters were visibly being constructed in the city. Mr. Le Vita, the inventor of the oxygen-supplied cradle in a suitcase, spoke eloquently to the most venerable public about his gas shelters for toddlers. Civil servants were lectured at work on how to avoid poisoning by deadly gases as membership dues for the Anti-Air Defense League were collected.

Having been persuaded to sign up for the League, he started to attend defense exercises, and had even conscientiously pulled on a pig-face gas mask, until reading in one of the opposition leaflets that such a gas mask was a highly dubious guarantee: it did not protect the whole body and was defenseless against mustard gas and lewisite; it did not produce oxygen and was useless in an atmosphere thick with gas; it was not universal, and the enemy was not in the habit of giving prior warning as to which gas it intended to use; finally, during the course of the war new gases would undoubtedly be introduced, ones not yet envisaged by the defense industry. The author of the leaflet argued most convincingly that only those countries occupying immense geographical expanses like the USSR would enjoy any protection from aerial gas attacks, while in countries that were territorially smaller, like Poland, the only effective means of defense was beating a hasty retreat, preferably in one's own car.

One day — the war was now raging in Abyssinia, while German outposts were already dotting the Rhine — he was enlisted to carry a stretcher during a practice gas attack. His partner was a bald, stout man who resembled an anteater in a snuff-colored jacket. The city seemed deserted. At the first wail of sirens the people reluctantly dragged themselves to the nearest gas shelters. Those who straggled were grabbed and hauled to the nearest sanitary station. To create the total illusion, the imaginary poison victims were ordered to stop up their mouth with a wet cloth, or otherwise a handful of dirt. People swore and spat. Assistance had to be called in to pacify others. The windows of the silenced flats shone with a deathly pallor, covered with crisscrosses of paper strips, as if they had been crossed out with chalk together with the inhabitants buried behind them.

By the end of the drills sweat was pouring off the hospital volunteers. Having removed the rubber trunk from his face, the bald man in the snuff-colored jacket panted and puffed and snorted. With his build such pursuits constituted certain asthma, and given a choice of the two evils, he would have preferred to have died from the gas than from the gas mask. The fat man was called Jagielski, and he served as the manager of one of the high-rent properties nearby. Jagielski invited his stretcher partner for a mug of beer to wet his parched throat. With this sort of anti-air defense there was no protecting yourself. Until recently, he had been forced to serve as an air defense superintendent for the whole building. The inhabitants had refused to adhere to any sort of discipline whatsoever. As a mark of protest, they refused to wash the pieces of paper from the windows, until finally threatened with a fine. During the recent night drills, when no light shed its rays onto the streets, the whole wall of the building had been plastered with anti-war proclamations. The communists had taken advantage of the darkness and adorned the whole district. Thankfully after this incident the son of the building's owner had assumed the superintendent responsibilities himself. He was welcome to them! As far as Mr. Jagielski was concerned, he would rather carry stretchers.

Over the beer it came out that Mr. Jagielski had been at the front during the German war and that the fuss over this new war did not agree with him at all. Maybe all this would still be settled somehow and the war wouldn't take place.

His stretcher partner turned out to be one of the pessimists. He looked at Jagielski with his glass eye and declared that war was a certainty. "They won't rest until they've killed us all!" He had been told this by a wise man who was never mistaken.

Another man, fidgeting in his lustrine coat, sat down at their table and expressed his interest in the name of the man who had so aptly formulated this truly remarkable thought. Learning that his name was Jan Głowak, the fidgety man expressed his regret that they were not acquainted and inquired after his place of residence. The gloomy interlocutor with a downcast eye said that Głowak had gone to where they all would eventually be sent — for a thinking man this was the only way out. The fidgety man gave a knowing wink, and from that moment became more conversational and frank. He, too, hated all this racket about the war.

Sober-minded people had to unite to get their say. In the course of the conversation he learned their names and where they worked ("having met clever men who think like me, I don't want to lose contact"). They exchanged firm handshakes and departed.

. . . During the night the pessimist with the glass eye was awoken by an unknown person standing in the middle of the room in an overcoat and fedora who ordered him to quickly gather his things. The response to his puzzled mutterings was that he had been arrested and that it would be useless to resist. Two other gentlemen disemboweled the furniture with a meticulous attention to detail. A policeman imposingly cleared his throat in the hall. A cabby was also waiting downstairs. The fiacre groaned under the weight of the passengers, yet took off at a pace that bounced off the cobblestones. The clatter of the horses' hoofs reverberated off the sleepy, silent walls.

In a certain establishment on Theater Square they diligently checked whether he remembered his name, his age, who his parents were, and what he did for a living. Then, with no transition whatsoever, just for good measure, they ordered him to name all the members known to him of the illegal anti-war organization to whose leadership he belonged, and to recount in more detail all he knew about one Jan Głowak and the links the organization was maintaining through him with a neighboring power.

He tried to assure them that Jan Głowak had hanged himself in 1920, but got punched in the mouth and flung against the wall. They gave him five minutes for reflection and offered a cigarette. When he had smoked it, they asked him once again to provide the names requested, and without any funny business. He again swore that there was no one for him to name. An athletic policeman told him to follow. Another policeman rose up from behind, then one more with prominent cheekbones in civilian clothes. In the doorway all three of them sized him up. A cold shiver ran down his spine. It was as if they already knew about his complex.

He was led into a windowless room, a solitary bench its only furnishing. He lost consciousness instantly from the forceful blow to the chin. He woke up on the floor — his knees tucked under his chin. He attempted to straighten up. His arms tightly clasped round his thighs began to ache from the handcuffs. He could not feel his own body; he rolled over into a circle, the axis of which was a wooden baton passed under his knees. An inhuman pain, as if they had picked at an inflammatory nerve. The pain returned to his head. He saw a policeman with rolled-up sleeves. The blow of a rubber truncheon . . . something once read, recalled from childhood: in China criminals were beaten on their heels with bamboo.

"What's your name?" sedately inquired both the officer with high cheekbones and the other policeman.

He shrank, trying to cross his legs under himself. Again a

terrible pain shot through him like an electric current, and he again lost consciousness.

By the end of the session he had named Jagielski, three clerks from the bank, and a cousin living in Kielce. He sobbed and pleaded for them to beat him no more — he really had forgotten the names of his other remaining acquaintances, but he would eventually remember, he would remember for sure and tell them. They freshened him up with water and took him barefoot to the cell: shoes do not fit on swollen, puffy feet.

At night he dreamed of the attack, the searchlights shone, and the officer who had damned him as a coward slowly unfastened his holster. He awoke agitated with his face covered in straw dust. Pressing himself into the bed, he tore at the pillow with his nails.

His whole body ached. How much time had passed since the interrogation? Days? At any moment they would call for him again. He had promised, or so it seemed, to provide some names. (The sound of footsteps boomed down the corridor). What names? Where was he to get them? (The steps thundered past. He gasped in relief.) Sooner or later this whole misunderstanding would resolve itself. They would come to realize that neither he nor any of the individuals he had named were in any way guilty. It was better to name anybody than to be beaten. He racked his brains in vain. It was only now that he realized just how unfortunately small his circle of acquaintances was. He could name the chief accountant, his wife's parents, but who else? He was not acquainted with the majority of the clerks and often confused their names. So who else? The bank director? They wouldn't believe him. And he could lose his job for that as well, so who else? His stomach started to ache from the strain. As there was no bucket to relieve himself within the cell he timidly tapped on the door. A silent sentry escorted him to the toilet, rattling his rifle. On the floor lay a crumbled piece of paper. He smoothed it out and mechanically cast a glance over the columns of tiny printed letters:

Mikolajczyk, Józef, barber, Krahmalnaya 1, 122974.

Miksta, Andrzej, lawyer, Nowy Świat 42, flat 17, 039843.

Mikulski, Foma, insurance agent, Kruglewska 23, flat 24, 051780.

He rolled his eyes lower: Mikulowski Jan, Mikulowski Kazimeirz, Milbark Franciszek . . . Milczek Wincenta . . . Mileiko Wiktor . . . Milewicz Ignacy . . . Milewski Stanisław . . . Milewski Alojzy . . . Milewski Zbigniew . . . Millenberg Izaak . . . Milski Bonifaty.

He froze for a moment with the paper in his hands. When he was certain the sentry was not looking he slipped it under his shirt.

For the whole of the following day, sitting on his bunk with his back to the door, and in a measured rocking movement, he mumbled in a sing-song voice, eyes closed: "Milewicz Ignacy, doctor, Nowolipki 18, flat 37 . . . Milewski Alojzy, funeral director, Old Town 6, courtyard . . . Milewski Stanisław, graphologist, Przejazd 12, flat 2 . . . Milewski Zbigniew . . ."

That night he was taken away for interrogation. He gave seven names, prudently retaining the remaining seven for the next time. He almost escaped without a beating.

The next time he named only four, keeping three in reserve just in case. He hadn't miscalculated. They called for him once again and thrashed him rather mercilessly. Obviously three surnames were not enough. But then, after the fourth interrogation, they left him alone. A couple of days later he was transferred to Mokotów Prison, to a solitary cell – number 212.

In prison there would be no more interrogations. Having recovered from the beatings and being convinced that they, evidently, were not going to beat him anymore, he began the patient wait for this whole misunderstanding to sort itself out, and for them to arrange his release. But days passed, then weeks, and nothing was resolved.

By the end of the second month he became agitated. Sitting on his bunk for days on end with nothing to do, he lost himself in reflection and conjecture. What did Milewski Alojzy, the owner of the funeral parlor, look like? Was he young or old? Judging by his business address and by the annotation "in the courtyard," he was hardly thriving. And Milewski Stanisław, the graphologist? He undoubtedly possessed a chic apartment. Flats with the number "2" were never higher than the first floor. Graphologists earned good money. What would he say when they came for him at night and ordered him to gather his things quickly? What was his wife living on now if she herself wasn't a graphologist?

By the end of the third month when the misunderstandings had not, as of old, sorted themselves out, the prisoner from cell 212 was overcome with pangs of conscience. He lost his appetite and stopped sleeping.

In the middle of the fourth month he conveyed via a guard that he wished to give the investigator some important evidence. When they brought him to the warden's office he told him unequivocally that all the testimony he'd given during the pre-liminary interrogations was false, not a single name was of an individual with whom he had ever been acquainted, he'd never seen them in the flesh and had no idea at all who they were.

The investigator put on his pince-nez, eyed the prisoner with an ironic look, and dryly said that evasion was pointless as all those named had fully admitted their guilt.

The prisoner from cell 212 closed his mouth and slowly trudged to the door, staring wide-eyed at the investigator.

The investigator added that the individuals in question had turned out to be more talkative than their ideological leader, and they had named a host of organization members he per-sonally had been unwilling to divulge. The court would not fail to take these extenuating circumstances into account. As far as the suspect was concerned, this belated attempt to deceive the organs of justice could only magnify his culpability and increase the severity of his sentence.

As he walked back to cell 212 the jailer was forced to sup-port him, holding his elbows and then pushing him forcefully through the appropriate doorway: the corridor swayed from side to side and the door to the cell appeared to be on the ceiling.

Toward the end of the eighth month a balding, pointy-nosed, middle-aged gentleman appeared at cell 212. He was dressed in a secondhand suit and carried a similarly shabby looking briefcase. He introduced himself to the prisoner as his court-appointed defense counsel and explained that the trial would begin in two weeks. It was time, as they say, to agree on the strategy they would adopt in court. The matter was totally clear, and as his defense attorney he had no need for any additional materials. He intended to construct his defense on the psychological plane, so to speak, appealing first and foremost to the patriotic sentiments of the judge. In this respect a decisive factor, and a positively winning one at that, was the defendant's participation in the Polish-Bolshevik War and his loss of an eye, so to say, for the sake of the motherland. His attorney intended to explain the defendant's transformation from valiant soldier and patriot to the ringleader of an illegal, anti-state organization as a product of his partial disability, as well as his having been subjected to foreign enemy influences. The chief defendant in this case should not be the accused himself, but his evil spirit, Jan Głowak, who had managed to exploit the defendant's instinctive hostility toward war, something any invalid would surely feel. The scoundrel Głowak, having sown discord in the soul of an honorable soldier, had escaped to the USSR, leaving behind his weak-willed victim to cook his own goose.

The defense attorney was convinced that after such an argument the judge would not dare to give him the death penalty and that the sentence would be a ten-year prison term. Everything depended on how he, the defendant, conducted himself during the trial. The case would undoubtedly attract a lot of publicity. What an understatement! Eighty in the dock! Anti-state elements would attempt to use the trial for their criminal pacifist agitations. It was extremely important, therefore, that the defendant's behavior in no way gave these elements any ammunition. It was essential for him to confirm all the evidence given at the preliminary hearing and to express, as his last word, heartfelt repentance and remorse. Only under these circumstances would the defense attorney take responsibility for the successful outcome of the trial. It was even possible that everyone would end up with something more like eight years rather than ten.

The conversation lasted about half an hour. The defense counsel did most of the talking. He left with a highly favorable impression of the defendant. He contradicted nothing, listened most attentively, and, as they said goodbye, emotionally extended his hand. At least that was how the defense attorney conveyed the conversation to the investigating officer and the public prosecutor.

Until the start of the trial the prisoner from cell 212 had conducted himself impeccably. On the day of the trial he was dressed in his own suit, was carefully shaved, and had been given a haircut. The prison barber, who had for some time worked in a provincial theater, splashed him from head to toe with eau de cologne and then stood back and spent a long time admiring the results.

The prison wagon was already waiting in the courtyard. They ceremoniously placed him inside with a twelve-man escort – policemen armed with rifles, polished as if on parade. The prison gate was thrown open and the vehicle solemnly rolled out toward town. It stopped several times en route, the noise and din of whistles piercing the air. The defendant attempted to look through the small grated window, but the twelve adjutants politely asked him to remain still. Once or twice he thought he clearly heard the sound of gunfire. Then the vehicle stopped. The doors were opened, and the retinue accompanied the defendant in rushing up the wide steps and into the court building.

As he was going up the steps, he looked around. In the

streets running from the square he saw a black sea of heads and the sky colored with the red stripes of placards. White foot-high letters shouted from one of the placards "Down with the warmongers!" The square was surrounded by black cordons of police, who cracked the safeties of their machine guns and pressed the crowd back into the streets.

He went cold in confusion, suddenly raising both arms and walking down the steps. Two policemen grabbed him under the arms and virtually at a gallop took him into the building.

The public had packed the large hall to overflowing. The hall suddenly began to murmur as he was led in and escorted to a place on the front bench. There were several rows of benches for the defendants, who sat there densely crammed and petrified. He stole a look at this unfamiliar crowd, at those to be tried with him. Jagielski's large bald patch shone dimly in the massed formation of the whiskered and the bearded and the clean shaven.

A bell tinkled. A resolute bass boomed "All rise for the judge!" All stood up and sat down on command. Then, like in the army, a roll call followed and everyone, each to their own tune, shouted out "present," whereupon a thin fellow with enormous ears got up from behind a table and started to read out all the charges. The reading took two and a quarter hours. The public yawned and picked their noses, while the dock listened with obvious, unflagging interest.

A strange transformation started to occur in the prisoner from cell 212. With all eyes in court trained on him during the reading of the vast philippic detailing his evil machinations as the ringleader and inspirer of this antiwar organization, incited by a neighboring power, he slowly stretched himself out as if he had grown by several inches, with the tilt of his head giving him a particularly proud bearing. Once or twice he openly surveyed the long rows of defendants, and his gaze — as was later confirmed by one of the ladies present — was somewhat that of a military leader surveying his troops. The features of his face became sharpened and enhanced — even his glass eye sparkled with an unusual gleam of excitement.

When the reading had abruptly concluded and the head of the court, having named the chief accused, asked if he would confess his guilt, the prisoner suddenly rose, and rather audibly, in a voice punctured by agitation, said:

"Yes, I admit my guilt! I am guilty of there being only eighty of us here. For in truth, there are many more of us, legions more! I understood this only today! None of us want war! We've had enough of living in the constant fear that you'll start killing us again, if not today, then tomorrow . . . !"

Pandemonium broke out. The old man behind the table made a prolonged attempt to cudgel the din with a bell, as if flailing it. Turning to the accused, he reminded him sternly that this was no communist rally, but a court of law. In the event of another such provocation he would be forced to have the prisoner removed. Deafened by the bell, the accused at once sank into his seat. The noise and ringing had clearly knocked all the elocution out of him, as if he had been choked by the very words. He looked indifferently at the pointy-nosed defense attorney, sadly nodding and wringing his hands in dismay.

Order was gradually restored. Those in the dock diligently confirmed, one by one, like schoolboys, "Yes, I confess." Among them were three with the surnames Milewski and Milski, but the prisoner from cell 212 did not even turn when he heard their names called.

Witness testimonies were given, then the court was adjourned.

As several newspapers noted, the crux of the case lay not so much in the speech of the chief suspect as in the unexpected statement of a defense counsel, Mikołajczyk, which occurred during the evening session. This defense counsel — a young attorney with no name to speak of, a man relatively unknown in the legal world — had drawn no one's attention during the whole course of the day's proceedings. During the witness testimonies he alone, from among the entire coterie of defense counselors, had failed to ask a single question, and only toward the end of the session did he approach the presiding judge for permission to ask the chief suspect a question.

He started by pointing out that upon examining the list of the accused, he had noticed one extremely strange coincidence: the surnames of fourteen of them all began with one and the same letter.

The judge shrugged his shoulders condescendingly. What was strange about the fact that fourteen out of the eighty members had a surname that began with the same letter? After all, the defense counsel could have developed this argument in his opening statement. Permission was granted only to put questions to the defendant.

The defense counsel gave his assurance that this was indeed what he intended to do; the coincidence to which he referred would not appear strange if the court had taken the trouble to open this very book, *The Warsaw Telephone Directory*, to page 217. The court would then have seen for itself that the surnames of all fourteen defendants were listed on this page successively, as telephone subscribers under the letter "M."

The defense counsel read aloud the surnames of all fourteen, with listed profession, address of domicile, and telephone number. Laughter rang through the court room. The judge reproachfully shook the bell.

Did it not seem strange that fourteen members of the accused's organization had been recruited straight from the telephone book? Could it be that the accused, understandably under duress during interrogation, had felt compelled to produce names of collaborators, and not having any at his disposal had picked them at random from the telephone book?

The laughter intensified. Now almost the whole room was in fits. Even the accused were smiling awkwardly.

The judge severely reprimanded the defense counsel for his inappropriate allusion to coerced interrogation methods, which by implication discredited the state's system of justice.

In order to put an end to the snickering, the judge turned to the accused and asked him sternly if what was being implied were true, that he had drawn the names of his fourteen accomplices from the telephone book.

The accused sat in embarrassed silence for a minute, eliciting another round of courtroom laughter, then he stood up and, turning red, uttered an emphatic "No!"

Sitting back down, he instantly went limp, his previous defiant bearing instantly vanishing. His right eye looked forward as motionless and vacantly as his left.

The counsel for the defense indicated that he had no further questions. The lively atmosphere that had gripped the courtroom did not subside.

The situation was saved by the public prosecutor, who requested that the trial be conducted behind closed doors since a number of testimonies touched on classified military secrets.

After a short adjournment, the court agreed to comply with the public prosecutor's recommendation.

The trial continued another three days, although neither the press nor the general public were to learn anything reliable about it. In trams and cafés information was passed in hushed tones: within 24 hours of the incident in court, sixty thousand customers of the Warsaw telephone company had withdrawn their subscriptions and requested their names be removed from the telephone directory. Seeing its very collapse on the horizon, the company, it was rumored, had appealed to the government with an urgent petition to acquit all of its subscribers. On the other hand, it was reported that military authorities were categorically pushing for all eighty accused to be found guilty so that it would set an example.

Judging by the sentencing, the matter ended in a compromise. The fourteen accused whose names began with "M" were found not guilty, the remainder sentenced to imprisonment of various lengths of time. Only the chief suspect was given the death penalty by hanging. Nevertheless, the head of state, having taken into consideration the convict's military past and his service in the defense of the resurrected Polish state, mitigated the punishment to death by firing squad.

The sentence was carried out on a February morning, so

uncommonly gloomy that the headlights of four cars had to be switched on. And when the Catholic priest approached the condemned man across the bare meadow ablaze with the glow of headlights and, shoving the cross under his nose, asked for his final wish, the condemned, dazzled by the light, answered most abstractedly: "I always knew that with just one eye there was no getting away from them! . . ."

1936

The present collection of Bruno Jasieński's shorter prose and manifestoes spans a brief but harrowing career, in two languages (Polish and Russian), across several countries (Poland, France, and Soviet Russia), accompanied by a slew of scandals and controversies and multiple shifts in aesthetics, persona, and political orientation. The selection has been made with an eye for providing a kind of overview of Jasieński's progress as a writer, through a period of history whose turbulence, particularly for an artist who enjoyed stirring up trouble, can scarcely be exaggerated.

"The Legs of Izolda Morgan" — which Jasieński introduces as a new form of "novel," in spite of its brevity — packs most of the major themes of the later novel *I Burn Paris* into its twenty-odd pages, and there is a crackle and spit to the writing that moves the plot forward with a kinetic irresistibility. The theme of society's treatment of the female body as a mechanism — and one which can be dismantled and adored in parts — is prefigured by the "To the Polish Nation" manifesto, which describes woman as the perfect machine and the ideal work of art. The suggestion is highly ambivalent. On the one hand, it predates feminism's insight of society's mechanization of the female body by about fifty years. On the other, we are reminded of cinema's proclivity for parsing the female body, presenting it in parts which are "severed," decontextualized, or expanded to gigantic proportions (in the close-up) for the erotic satisfaction of audiences. Berg's obsession with Izolda's legs only shifts this cinematic fetish. Film critic Siegfried Kracauer once wrote that the power of the cinematic fragment is in how it leaves us longing for and anticipating the larger whole; Berg's case, however, represents a reversal. His possession of Izolda's legs is fulfillment enough – the rest of the body swiftly turns out to be a useless appendage, beneath his attention. Yet like any great writer, Jasieński's politics consistently undermine themselves, rendering any conclusive reading disturbingly elusive. By the novella's end it is impossible to say where it is set: in Berg's deranged mind, in a world run amok, or perhaps the distinction has become entirely irrelevant.

"Keys," written in 1925 when Jasieński was twenty-four years old, forms a bridge of sorts from his Futurist period to his later satirical work. Instead of the page-long sentences it has a staccato, almost perfunctory feel, and until recently it had been omitted from Polish anthologies of his work. Nonetheless, its attack on religious hypocrisy was quite bold in the arch-Catholic Poland of the 1920s, and its tone of moral outrage anticipates his later work. The more laconic the prose becomes, the more appalling the narrative. The effect is somewhat complex – in giving an absurdly terse commentary on the events, the narrator creates the impression of a world where ethical insanity is met with complicity or bland indifference. This implicit worldview is one of the few constants in Jasieński's highly varied oeuvre.

The two novellas "The Nose" and "The Chief Culprit" were both written in Russian in 1936 when Jasieński was living in Moscow. Composed around the time when Stalin's Great Purge was getting underway, they are examples of how "officially sanctioned" themes could be used to subversive and defiantly *literary* ends. Though Jasieński was known as a firebrand, and there is evidence that he was involved in denouncing other writers, it should be remembered that as a high-profile Pole — albeit one who had repeatedly attacked his home country's sacred cows and who was now writing in Russian and supporting the Soviet cause — he would have been a natural target for persecution (no one knows how many Poles died as a result of the Great Purge, but the number is estimated to be in the hundreds of thousands). Thus the themes of these novellas are "safe": the evil of Nazi Germany's racial policies and the dehumanization of life in Poland's army, legal system, and society at large. What keeps these texts from becoming heavy-handed or didactic, however, is Jasieński's evident glee in skewering his targets.

"The Nose" advertises its indebtedness to Gogol in the title and epigraph, and can very well be read as a fantasia on the idea of Gogol's runaway nose infecting the world to a murderous and brutal extent married to the Nazi obsession for phrenological research and physiological classification. What *does* it mean, after all, that a man lives or dies for the shape of his nose? In Gogol's famous story, the nose grows to vast proportions, is clothed in noble robes, and acquires, literally, a life of its own. Jasieński's story describes a similar phenomenon, with a great scrupulousness to historical fact — the various cited academics and scientists and their work are as genuine as they are bizarre.

One finds an analogy for "The Chief Culprit" in Nathanael West's *A Cool Million: The Dismantling of Lemuel Pitkin*, which, as in Jasieński's story, takes the physical mutilation of a young, bright-eyed naif to hideous extremes. The protagonist learns that the mundane life he once knew, his work in the bank, was at best an illusion, and that the real substance of life in a capitalist society rears its murderous head in times of war and in endless preparation for the war to come — and one is always on the horizon. Jasieński's message that in modern war the ordinary civilian is the "chief culprit" — and thus the primary enemy — naturally has its antecedents and only became more relevant with the increasing destructive power of weaponry. The fantasy cities to help citizens survive modern warfare are obviously satire, but they also harken back to a pre-modern world where towns were *created* as defensive structures. What has changed in the meantime are the weapons themselves, which require the city of the future to take more fantastic precautions.

In the early 1920s, avant-garde manifestoes flashed into existence and expired, one after another, at a furious pace. The two included here are foundational to the Polish Futurist movement and display the phonetic, "barbaric" approach to spelling. For "Nife in the Gutt" I have attempted to render Jasieński's phoneticizations and deliberate misspellings in a reasonable English equivalent that is nevertheless, hopefully, intelligible. After consulting with the editor, I decided to translate "To the Polish Nation" without the Futurist spellings but with the conviction that the content deserves clarity and a reader whose attention is not focused on spelling. It is probably fair to say that this mangling of language would have been considered just as controversial as the contents of the manifestoes themselves, but it was also unmistakably a declaration. A revolution in art demanded a whole new approach to language, and if some might find the solution in these manifestoes unpleasantly literal, it was a mandate that Jasieński carried over into "The Legs of Izolda Morgan" and *I Burn Paris* in a much more compelling and intricate form.

This volume contains most of the shorter prose Jasieński committed to paper in Russian and in Polish; omitted are a few short manifestoes that too specifically target the Polish language (and its mutilation) to be of much use to the English-language reader, and one story in Russian entitled "Bravery," whose propagandistic qualities outweigh its literary merits. He also wrote a pair of novels in Russian, one of which was left unfinished. It is a rare pleasure as a translator to wish that a writer had had time to write more, to feel unsated with the remaining work to translate, to be actually left with the sensation that he will *miss* translating this author.

Invaluable contributions to the translations were made by Marcin Piekoszewski (for "The Legs of Izolda Morgan") and Howard Sidenberg (throughout). I am also grateful to my co-translator, Guy Torr, for his enthusiasm and skill in taking on Jasieński's Russian texts.

Soren Gauger
Krakow, 2014

A NOTE ON THE TEXTS

The present volume comprises work Bruno Jasieński wrote both in Polish in the 1920s during and immediately after his Futurist period (translated by Soren Gauger), and in Russian after resettling in the Soviet Union in 1929 (translated by Guy Torr).

BIBLIOGRAPHY

"To the Polish Nation: A Manifesto on the Immediate Futurization of Life" originally appeared in Polish as "Do narodu Polskiego. Mańifest w sprawie natyhmiastowej futuryzacji żyća," (Krakow, April 20, 1921) and published in *Jednodniówka futurystów* (Krakow, June 1921); reprinted in *Antologia polskiego futuryzmu i Nowej Sztuki* (Wrocław: Biblioteka Narodowa, 1978) and in *Nogi Izoldy Morgan* (Warsaw: Jirafa Roja, 2005).

"Nife in the Gutt: 2nd Phuturist Pamflet" originally appeared in Polish as "Nuż w bżuhu: 2. jednodńuwka futurystuw," printed as a broadside and made public on November 13, 1921. Reprinted in *Antologia polskiego futuryzmu i Nowej Sztuki* (Wrocław: Biblioteka Narodowa, 1978).

"The Legs of Izolda Morgan" originally appeared in Polish as *Nogi Izoldy Morgan* (Odrodzenie: Lwów, 1923); reprinted in *Nogi Izoldy Morgan i inne utwory* (Warsaw: Czytelnik, 1966) and in *Nogi Izoldy Morgan* (Warsaw: Jirafa Roja, 2005).

"Polish Futurism (An Accounting)" originally appeared in Polish as "Futuryzm polski (bilans)," in *Zwrotnica*, no. 6 (1923); reprinted in *Antologia polskiego futuryzmu i Nowej Sztuki* (Wrocław: Biblioteka Narodowa, 1978).

"Keys" originally appeared in Polish as "Klucze" in *Torpeda* (Lwów, 1925); reprinted in *Nogi Izoldy Morgan* (Warsaw: Jirafa Roja, 2005).

"The Nose" was originally published in Russian as "HOC" in *Sovetskii Pisatel* (Moscow, 1936); reprinted in Polish as "Nos" in *Nogi Izoldy Morgan i inne utwory* (Warsaw: Czytelnik, 1966) and in *Nogi Izoldy Morgan* (Warsaw: Jirafa Roja, 2005).

"The Chief Culprit" was originally written in Russian as "ГЛАВНЫЙ ВИНОВНИК" and first published in Polish in 1957 as "Główny winowajca"; reprinted in *Nogi Izoldy Morgan i inne utwory* (Warsaw: Czytelnik, 1966).

ABOUT THE AUTHOR

Poet, novelist, and playwright, Bruno Jasieński was born in Klimontów, Poland, in 1901. Having authored in 1921 "To the Polish Nation: A Manifesto on the Immediate Futurization of Life" and "Manifesto on Futurist Poetry" he became the unquestionable leader of Polish Futurism, writing poetry that was marked by dynamism and absurdity. In 1925, he emigrated to France but was deported after his novel *I Burn Paris* was serialized in 1928. He spent the last decade of his life in the USSR working for the Union of Soviet Writers and producing work in Russian, chief among which were the play *The Mannequins' Ball* (1931) and the novel *Man Sheds His Skin* (1934). Arrested in 1937, Jasieński was expelled from the Party, put on trial, and sentenced to fifteen years in the gulag. Thought for many years to have died in transit sometime in 1939, it is now known that he was executed on September 17, 1938, in Moscow's Butyrka prison. The Brunonalia Festival is held annually in his honor in Klimontów.

ABOUT THE TRANSLATORS

Soren A. Gauger is from Vancouver, Canada, and has resided in Krakow for over a decade. His translations include *Waiting for the Dog to Sleep* by Jerzy Ficowski, *Towers of Stone* by Wojciech Jagielski, and Bruno Jasieński's novel *I Burn Paris*. His own writing has appeared in numerous journals and includes a collection of stories, *Hymns to Millionaires*, and a forthcoming novel.

Guy Torr lives and works in Krakow where he is a senior lecturer in English Language at Jagiellonian University. A contributor to the *Wielki słownik polsko-angielski* (2004) and Larousse's *Praktyka metoda nauki słownictwa* (2005), since 1996 he has worked as a Russian-Polish-English translator for the trilingual lexicon of Russian thought *Ideas in Russia,* published by the University of Łódź, as well as contributed a number of papers on Chekhov in English.

Bruno Jasieński
THE LEGS OF IZOLDA MORGAN
Selected Writings

Translated by Soren A. Gauger from the original Polish
and Guy Torr from the original Russian

To the editors of *Sein und Werden* our gratitude for
publishing an earlier version of "Polish Futurism"

Cover by Dan Mayer
Design by Silk Mountain
Text set in Garamond, titles in Univers

Frontispiece: Portrait of Bruno Jasieński
by Stanisław Ignacy Witkiewicz, pastel on paper, 1923,
courtesy of the Museum of Literature, Warsaw

FIRST EDITION

Published in 2014 by
TWISTED SPOON PRESS
P.O. Box 21 – Preslova 12
150 21 Prague 5, Czech Republic
www.twistedspoon.com

Printed and bound in the Czech Republic by Akcent

Distributed in the U.K. and Europe by
CENTRAL BOOKS
99 Wallis Road
London, E9 5LN
United Kingdom
www.centralbooks.com